BROKEN

KING BROTHERS BOOK THREE

LISA LANG BLAKENEY

WRITERGIRL PRESS

To Every English Teacher Who Told Me I Should Write
Thank you

First he lied to me.
Then he seduced me.
Now he's broken me.

I knew him as a boy, but now the boy is back—a hardened criminal.
Big as hell. Blindingly beautiful. Sexy as sin.
Dripping with attitude. Covered in ink.
And carrying a colossal chip on his shoulder.

I want to keep my distance.
Needing to protect myself and my virginity.
He's awakening parts of me that I never knew were dormant.
Ruining me for any other man.

I should have known that nothing this good would be healthy for me.
He's a liar. A thief. A convict. A deviant.

I need to walk away from this man who's breaking me piece by piece.
Only my heart is not cooperating.

ONE

STONE

Visiting Room
White Pines Penitentiary
White Pines Village, New York

"I don't usually accept visits from strangers."

I stare menacingly at the vertically challenged man wearing a black cloth patch across a missing eye as he sits down. He looks like a short pirate in a three-piece suit.

"Correction, you don't take visits from anyone."

I narrow my eyes and take a longer look at my visitor. He's been doing his homework on me which means he wants something. Anyone who takes an interest in me wants something.

"How would you know that."

"I know a lot about you, Michael Barringer, and it's time that you know a bit about me too. The name's Silas Buckshot Porter. Most people call me Bucky, and I'm the man you stole seven million dollars' worth of heroin from."

Fuck me.

So, this is him.

I'm serving time in prison, because I was caught in possession of a large quantity of heroin with an intent to distribute. This man's heroin.

I've been watching my back inside of these prison walls for five years. Waiting for some connection he may have inside to make their move on me in retaliation, but no one ever did. I thought maybe I got away with it. That I was all good. But it's in this exact moment that I'm realizing that was a mistake. I let my guard down. Only now am I remembering and understanding what my father always told me.

There's no way to avoid the wrath of the devil, Stone. When he comes, he comes, and you just better be prepared to deal with the motherfucker.

"So, it was your product."

"Not even going to pretend that you didn't take it, huh?"

"Nope. I definitely took that shit and it was real easy."

He grins baring a set of perfect white teeth.

"I like that about you. You've got balls. May I ask what made you target my shipment in particular?"

"No reason."

He smooths the lapels of his jacket.

"I don't think that's true, Mr. Barringer. I think you targeted me specifically, because that seems to be your pattern. You stole from a few other people I know. You have a particular hard-on for heroin dealers."

"You do realize that our conversations are being monitored, right?"

He chuckles.

"If I was worried about that I wouldn't be here. The difference between you and me is that I have connections that you don't. That you'll never have. That's why you're in here and I'm out there. You'd do best to remember that."

"I'm getting tired of this fucking conversation. Say what you came here to say and leave."

"All right–"

He leans in farther toward me.

"You took seven million dollars from me, and I want it back."

"I don't have it."

"You're going to get it."

"I'm not–"

"You know how I got to where I am, Mr. Barringer? I served my country flying supply planes from the states for army rangers."

Alarms go off in my head when he says army rangers. My adoptive father, Jack, was an army ranger, but I'm not going to let this guy know that what he's saying means anything to me.

"And."

"And I knew your foster dad or sorry...adoptive father, Jack."

I don't move a muscle in my face.

"Your father and a man named Nathan Carter and I had a deal back in the old days. We were all partners."

"That's bullshit. My father was a stone mason."

"Come on now, you think you and Jack lived in the ritzy part of Brooklyn off of a mason's income? Hell fucking no. Your father made his money with me back when we were rangers. I moved a lot of heroin in those planes I flew and he helped me. The split was fifty-fifty. I got fifty percent for transporting it and your father, and Nate split their half for helping me get it on the plane."

"Even if I were to believe this tall tale of yours, if you think Jack left me a lot of money when he died, let me assure you that he didn't. Just a small life insurance policy.

If he had the type of money you're talking about, I would have known."

"You're one lucky son of a bitch, do you know that? If you were anyone else, you would have been dead the first thirty days of your stay in this steel cage. But seeing that your father saved my ass once or twice when I was young and dumb, I'm going to give you an opportunity to redeem yourself. I know Jack didn't have any money when he died. I knew everything about Jack. He had a gambling problem and a woman problem. He spent way too much money on craps and beer and pussy."

I tighten my fist that's resting on the table between us.

Jack was a good man, and I won't tolerate anyone telling me any different.

"Listen up—"

"No, you listen, Mr. Barringer. Our other partner, Nate, probably still has his money and the sweet thing is, is that I don't owe that son of a bitch shit. You're going to get it from him, or I promise you that you're dead the second you step out of this prison."

I stare at the one-eyed devil in his one good eye and can see that he means exactly what he says. I didn't protect my ass literally and figuratively in this place for five years to die.

"I haven't seen Nate since my father's funeral, but when I did he certainly didn't seem like he was rolling in it."

"What made us good at what we did is that we never brought attention to ourselves. You never even heard of me, right? That's because I keep a low profile. I'm way under the radar. So is Nate. Trust me when I say that he has some money stashed somewhere, and you better hope that it's at least seven million dollars."

"And how do you propose I steal this imaginary money?"

"You're a professional thief, Mr. Barringer. Do what you do best. Lie."

I slam my hands flat on the table in frustration garnering the attention of a couple of guards.

"Keep it down, Barringer," one of them warns me.

"I steal drugs from drug dealers," I say through clenched teeth. "I don't steal money from my father's friends."

"Drugs are money, Mr. Barringer. My money. Listen, I realize that you have some sort of Robin Hood fetish. I don't know why. Maybe you heard that your biological mama was a heroin addict or maybe a few of those kids in the foster home overdosed on some bad smack? Whatever the reason, that seems to be why you steal from businessmen like myself that only deal in heroin, and then you flush it down the toilet or some ridiculous shit like that. Do you think you're making a difference? Hurting us? Well here's the reality check. You aren't making a dent in my business. You aren't stopping anything. You're just making things difficult for yourself."

"If I wasn't making a difference, you wouldn't be here now would you."

He tightens his tie.

His voice rises an octave.

"You make zero difference. Trust and believe that. But I have a business to run and I can't let a theft like yours go unchecked. It sets a bad example for the other brazen dick-heads out in the world like you."

He takes a deep breath like he's attempting to center himself.

"Listen, I don't want to argue. In fact, I'm going to be a nice guy and give you options. You see just like you, Nate took something from me a long time ago, and I never forget a debt. He owes me. So, you can either steal the seven million dollars you owe me from him or you can steal something else even more precious of his."

"What."

"His daughter."

"What?"

"Make her fall in love with you then break her."

This motherfucker is crazy.

"I'm not doing that shit."

"It's either that, my money, or your death, Mr. Barringer. Any one of those will satisfy your debt. The choice is yours."

TWO

STONE

FEBRUARY

My name is Michael Blackwood Barringer, but everyone calls me Stone. The story around the origins of my nickname isn't particularly creative or unique. The way I heard it, it was simply because I was a very big kid. Heavy as a rock to carry. Hard as a boulder to move. Therefore, I was given the nickname Stone.

The name stuck with me through my younger years in elementary school and into adulthood, not just because of my size, but because no one could really read my emotions.

Kids called me Stone, because they didn't dare call me anything else. They were mostly frightened of me and rightly so. I was tall and muscular for my age and often used it to my advantage. Starting fights. Breaking up fights.

There were also a couple of teachers who used the nickname as well. They would often say that I was unreadable or unapproachable, because I wore a "stoned face" throughout the day. I think that even one or two of them wanted to get me tested at one point for a personality disorder.

I'm sure that if I had been a cute little girl, with ringlets, and a big grin across my face all the time, those same teachers would have discovered that I wasn't some damaged or flawed kid, but that actually I was pretty intelligent for my age. Smart but bored. Unfortunately, most of my mediocre teachers couldn't get past the fact that I was bigger than them, stronger than them, and quieter than most. They didn't realize I had a brain, and I'm not even sure how much they would have cared even if they had known. I don't bring out the nurturing instinct in people. I bring out the urge to fight or take flight.

For the five years that I served as a prisoner in the New York State penal system, I was also known as Stone or inmate 745924. I served my time quietly and without any real serious issues. Sure, there were definitely times when I had to prove that I was the wrong one to fuck with, but unlike the many prison television shows and movies depicting horrible daily violence such as murder and rape, jail was actually pretty damn boring.

Day in and day out, it was the same routine for mostly every man there. Everyone who isn't serving life in prison, just wants to serve their time quietly so that they can make parole. I was no different. I served my predictable and ritualistic sentence one month, one week, and one day at a time. Biding my time. And that time has finally come.

I was released this morning after serving five of my seven year prison sentence with an early probation under specific conditions. When felons like me are released under a court agreement, someone has to vouch for them. They need to vouch that I won't leave the state in which I committed the crime (New York). Vouch that I'll meet with my assigned probation officer regularly. And vouch that I won't be a menace to the community and actually become a productive member of society.

Because I was an exemplary prisoner, and have no real home to call my own in New York, the court was willing to grant me a parole transfer to another state and place me under the supervision of the one person I needed to put a roof over my head and that's Nate Carson.

Nate isn't my family by blood. Actually, I don't know if I have any blood relatives to speak of. Never cared to find out. If they don't give a damn about me, why should I give a rat's ass about them? Nate Carson was the best friend of my adoptive father, Jack. They were very close. Served over twenty-two years as rangers in the army together.

When I was just a kid, and Jack and I still lived in Pennsylvania, we spent a lot of time over at Nate's house. Sometimes we'd have Chinese takeout together, while they taught me how to play poker. Other times we'd watch a ballgame, while I eagerly listened to many of their old army tales. And then a few times it was obvious that we were over there, so that they could make me babysit while they grabbed a couple of brews at the local pub. That's how I first met Nate's only daughter.

While it wasn't my idea of a good time at that age, I actually didn't mind watching the soft-spoken little bookworm for a couple of hours while the two of them caught up. It made Jack happy, and if anyone deserved some moments of happiness, it was Jack.

He'd had a hard as nails life, which was one of the reasons why he seemed to be so drawn to me. I'd had one too. Both of his parents were addicts and he was raised by his grandmother and welfare. After she passed, he enrolled in the army looking for somewhere to belong. For someone to give a damn about him. That's what he said he found during his time in the armed forces. A family.

I think because of all of that, Jack wanted to save me too, and in many ways, he did. I was the little boy in the foster home that no one wanted to adopt. I was too quiet. Too big. Too old. Too much of a wildcard. When I finally moved in with him, I was also too much of a pain in the ass. I acted out. I pushed him. I tested my boundaries. It was all because I didn't trust that Jack could love me. I didn't think I was worthy of it. If my own parents threw me away, then what would this surly old army ranger want with me.

But he did want me. Probably the only person that ever did or ever would. So, in my eyes, Jack was a saint. A saint who left this earth too soon. I still to this day don't know how to really deal with the fact that he's gone. I don't think anyone can teach you how to move on from the biggest loss of your life. You just have to try. In any and all of the ways that you can, because the alternative is to just lay down and die.

And I sure as shit ain't dying.

So here I am.

Headed south toward Philadelphia, on the New Jersey Turnpike, in Nate's Chevy pickup. Calculating how long it will take me to figure out if he has money and if he does where it is, before I can get the fuck out of Dodge for good.

I feel an emotion that is so foreign to me when I look over at Nate. Guilt. Like a small pebble stuck in my throat. Probably because he looks so happy.

He thinks he's doing his old friend Jack a favor by taking in his son. He thinks I'm getting my shit together. He thinks I'm a good kid that's just been dealt a terrible hand in life. And while it's accurate that I have been dealt a fucked-up hand...the real truth is that *I'm* just plain ole' fucked-up.

THREE

TINY

I twirl a little piece of heaven around my fork, slide it in my mouth, and close my eyes to savor it. There's nothing like a helping of freshly made anchovy pasta. Pasta cooked al dente, mixed with anchovy and Roma tomato pasta sauce, and topped with a little arugula and Romano cheese. It's a simple, authentic, Italian dish that makes my mouth water and almost brings tears to my eyes.

My name is Ariana Carter, known to close friends and family as Tiny, and exclusively to my father as baby girl. Enjoying good food is almost like a spiritual experience for me. In another life, I would have been a food critic, traveling the world trying dishes from all over, and then writing about what did or what didn't make the dish special. Too bad I can't write.

Instead I have a much different career that thankfully doesn't involve the written word. I make a great living as a registered ER nurse at Pennsylvania Memorial Hospital. It's a meaningful career which impacts lives, pays well, and luckily for me is in demand all over the world.

Today I'm out for a late lunch with my ex, Doctor Bill

Rappaport, at one of my favorite Italian restaurants–Trattoria. A small place under the radar with fresh ingredients and superior customer service. I asked him here because I need a favor, not because I'm trying to rekindle anything between us, because that would be absolute insanity on my part.

Bill definitely doesn't want to be in a relationship. In fact, I'm not even really sure what Bill wants. We rarely went on actual dates, he hardly ever called, he didn't want people at the hospital to know we were dating, and we never even had sex. He doesn't even know that I'm a twenty-five-year-old virgin, because the subject didn't even come up. Frankly, I'm not sure that the man ever even liked me, and the whole relationship has me second-guessing myself at every turn. It was a complete confidence crusher.

"I think it's safe to say that you like the pasta," he says with a fair amount of snark to his comment. Reminding me yet again of another one of his unfavorable traits. Making passive aggressive comments about my relationship with food.

"What's that supposed to mean?" I challenge. "Don't you like your meal?"

"I don't even know. I was too busy staring at you eat yours."

I quickly remember what I'm here for, and it's not to get into some sort of pissing match with Bill about what I eat or the way that I eat. I really could give two shits about what he thinks. Those days are thankfully over. I roll my eyes and then look away from him for a moment wiping the corner of my mouth with my napkin.

Don't kick him in the shin under the table. Remember why you're here.

"I didn't mean anything by it, babe. It's just the cardiologist in me. You wouldn't understand."

Another thing about Bill I don't like. I know, the list is kind of long. Always throwing up the fact that he's a doctor and I'm a nurse in a derogatory way. As if I took the "easy" way out. As if I'm lesser than him. Never mind that nurses do all the heavy lifting in every hospital all over the world, and the doctors get paid twice as much as us to "supervise" the work that we do. Work in my opinion that they should be doing too.

"Yeah, I'm pretty sure that I already know what you meant by it. Let's drop it," I say. "That's not what I asked you here for."

"This meeting isn't about us?" he asks as if he can't believe I would want something from him other than pursuing a reconciliation. As if I'd ever do that.

"No, Bill." I sigh.

"Oh, I thought you might have been a little lonely tonight. Maybe wanted some company." He grins. "I know you typically spend the Friday nights that you're not working curled up with one of those dirty books of yours."

"What are you my grandma? They're called romance novels and no, this isn't about a booty call. I asked you here to talk about your sister's agency."

It's time I get to the point of this dinner, because he's getting on my nerves and I really need to dine and dash anyway. I promised to be home by at least seven.

"The agency?"

"Yeah, I'm thinking about applying for a traveling nurse assignment."

Bill raises one of his eyebrows. "Really?"

"Yes, really."

"You're going to leave your dad to ramble around in that house by himself?"

Another dig at the fact that I still live at home with my father. Something I've never felt I had to explain to anyone until I started messing around with Bill, but now have begun to question myself. Not because I don't think a woman in her twenties can't live with her parents, but because my house is actually a difficult place for me to live in.

Every corner.

Every closet.

Every hallway.

Every picture on the wall reminds me of my mom and makes me extremely nostalgic and terribly sad. I miss her in a way that must be different for my father. While he chooses to live deep in a life full of constant memories and reminders of her, those same memories are crushing me. I feel like I am literally being smothered by all of the reminders of my mother in this house. That's why I'm looking for a traveling nurse placement. I need to get out of there before I suffocate.

"Are you going to tell me about the agency or not, Bill."

"All right, all right. You're so touchy tonight. Are you on your period?"

"Bill!" I exclaim. Completely exasperated with him in the all of forty minutes we've been in each other's company.

"Fine. My sister Stephanie is the one with the agency. She's been a nurse for over thirty-five years and opened the agency about twelve years ago. A lot of good nurses have come through there."

"Your older sister, right?"

"Yeah, the one who lives in Merion with my oldest nephew, Josiah. The one who plays soccer."

"Yes, I remember you talking about them. I really like that an experienced nurse owns the agency and not just an administrative person."

"Right, well she has a lot of solid relationships with human resource departments at every hospital within a fifty mile radius of Philly. Thanks to me of course."

"Of course." I roll my eyes.

"So, she should be able to find you a good assignment. I'll actually see her over the weekend at a family thing. I'll mention to her that you're looking. Where are you thinking about going?"

"Maybe out west or even down south. I just kind of want to stretch my legs. Get out of the metro area for a while and see what's out there."

"You've never lived outside of Philly, right?"

Yet another subtle jab.

He's on a roll tonight.

"You know that I haven't, Bill. I went to U Penn straight after high school and then started working at Memorial three weeks after graduation."

I take another forceful bite of my pasta and eat it with angry swallows.

"Would it be a little inappropriate to say that I hope things don't work out for you? I mean I'd hate to see you go."

"Yes, Bill, that would be totally inappropriate to say and selfish as hell."

His phone vibrates on top of the table. Disrupting our conversation. Thank God.

"Sorry about this. I'm on call."

"No problem. Take it."

I'm used to it. Bill is always on call. Even when he was off shift and hanging out with me, his mind was always at the hospital.

"Dammit, I've got to go. Some guy just came in with a steel rod in his chest. Punctured his heart."

"Not a problem. Sounds like your type of case."

"Actually, I think it may be kind of a problem. It took me a month to even get you to talk to me again, and now I have to go. I'm afraid that you won't talk to me for another month now that you've gotten what you wanted out of me."

"What are you talking about. I'm just following the rules that you laid out between us. No personal chitchat in the workplace. No exposing our relationship to coworkers. Etcetera, etcetera."

"It was the professional thing to do. We'd have been such a cliché if everyone knew. The doctor and the nurse having a thing," he says while he obnoxiously snaps to grab the attention of our server.

A *thing* is just about all it was between us. It wasn't even worth mentioning to my coworkers, but that's not the point. He was keeping our relationship hidden like it was some dirty little secret. The jerk.

"I'll text you my sister's information later, and give her a heads-up to expect your call."

The server still hasn't come to our table, so he dramatically drops several twenty-dollar bills on the table to cover the bill as if it's some grand gesture.

"We can split the check you know," I say flatly. Wondering if asking him for this favor was even worth the trouble.

"Don't insult me. You know I've got it."

After he leaves, I'm relieved because that means I get to polish off my bowl of pasta and my remaining glass of wine without judgment.

My judgment in men truly stinks. I'm always *just*

friends with all the good ones, like my pal Jagger from Penn, and attracted to the losers.

I check the time and decide to turn down the offer to look at the dessert menu and head home instead. My father should be arriving back soon with our new guest, and I need to straighten up the place among other things. I'm a little anxious about this visitor.

Stone Barringer.

Family friend turned bad boy turned hardened criminal, and now he's coming to live with us after his release from prison. Mr. Jack's son or not, I made sure to share with my father just how much I don't agree with this living arrangement.

Honestly, I barely remember Mr. Jack and certainly don't remember much about his son. Why my father feels like he has to do this is beyond me. It's not smart and it's not safe.

I get about two blocks from the restaurant when I hear the blaring sound of a police siren behind me. I look in my rearview window, wondering if I need to pull over, so that the car can get by me to continue their pursuit. I definitely don't want to be rear-ended by a police cruiser.

I slow down and swerve over toward the side of the road, but when I do, I become thoroughly confused when the police car pulls directly behind me and stops.

Are they stopping me?

FOUR

STONE

"You hungry?" Nate asks turning down the music in the car. His voice sounds a little funny. Like it hurts for him to speak. Almost in the same way after someone's been slowing squeezing your windpipe. I've given a couple dudes that experience firsthand.

"Nah, not really."

I'm lying right now. I'm a big boy, so I'm actually always hungry, but I don't want Nate thinking that he has to house me *and* feed me. That's just asking for entirely too much. Like I'm staying in some sort of free bed and breakfast for fuck ups.

"All right." He coughs a couple of times and then turns the music back up after a moment of awkward silence.

It's not good for my plan that the two of us are walking on egg shells around each other. I'm not going to get him to reveal any financial secrets like this. I'm not sure what's going on with Nate. This isn't the way I remember him being with me when I was a kid. It was easier then. Probably because we don't really know how to interact around each other any longer. It's been a long time.

Jack and I moved to New York when I was a kid. He had to move for work as a mason, which always kept him busy (at least that's what I thought was keeping him busy), so we didn't get back to Philly too much. I can't remember the last time I saw him prior to Jack's funeral. I just know that when I did, I was basically still a boy. Now I've returned a man.

A very fucked-up man.

I'm sure that part of the weirdness between us is that I've been in prison for five years, and people have their preconceived notions about what prison is like. About what it does to a man. It would be natural for Nate to have those sorts of thoughts about me. Those questions. Those assumptions. I get it and I certainly don't blame him. I don't blame anyone but myself. Besides, some of those preconceived notions are actually right on the money.

"So, I'll be staying in your daughter's old room?" I ask in an effort to make this painful ass car ride a little easier. From what I remember, Nate loves talking about his daughter. She was the center of his world back then. Can't imagine much has changed now. That's probably why that asshole Bucky brought her into this.

"Old room?" He roughly clears his throat. Something he's done ten or fifteen times since we've been in the car. I thought it was some sort of weird tic of his at first. Now I realize it's because he's sick.

"Yeah, isn't she away at school?"

Nate smirks. "I know you haven't seen her in years, but I think you forget that my daughter isn't that much younger than you. She's out of school and working."

Time flies when you're living recklessly.

"What does she do?" I ask. Curious as to the woman she's grown to be. All I remember is a quiet little girl who used to pretend she was a Powerpuff Girl when she thought no one was looking.

"My baby girl is a nurse," Nate says proudly. "After she graduated Penn she moved back in with me. She gets to save money this way, and I get the comforts of still having a woman around. She keeps the place clean and cooks most nights. I'm definitely blessed."

I didn't even think to question if Nate's daughter was still living at home. I bet that Bucky already knew that.

"You didn't mention she was living with you."

"I didn't?" He smirks as he continues to drive. "Guess I just assumed you already knew. Thought you might have been keeping tabs on us over the years. You know you kids are all on social media and stuff."

"I don't do social media."

Living with Nate is one thing, but living with both of them is something else. It puts her directly next to me, in Bucky's path, which means she's in considerable danger.

Of course, there's nothing I can do about it now. I made a deal with the devil to save my ass, so I've got to make it work or risk seeing Jack and the man upstairs much earlier than I anticipated, and that shit–is not happening.

"Does she know I'm coming?"

He gives me a momentary glance.

"Of course, she does. She's probably even cooking up something special for your arrival."

"I hope she isn't," I mutter under my breath.

Hey, you know what's funny," he says. "When she was little, especially after I lost my sweet Joanne, I would worry about her constantly. Worry that I wasn't teaching her everything she needed to know about life. All the things a girl needs to know. At least in the way that Jo would have taught her. Especially about boys and all of that."

"Uh huh."

"Your father knew I was struggling with that. That's why the two of us made a pact. Jack and I went through a lot when we did our tour in the Gulf. We learned a lot of hard lessons. There's a little bit of evil in almost everyone, and the world is a cruel and crazy place. As you and I both know so painfully well, tomorrow isn't guaranteed. We've both lost people who we loved. That's why your father and I promised each other that we'd raise you two like blood. Raise you to take care of each other. It gave us peace of mind knowing that when this world took us you two would have each other."

I lower my head quietly. I perfected this in prison. The art of being quiet. I don't want to say out loud what I'm thinking. I can't. That pebble of guilt is rolling around the base of my throat. Making it hard to speak.

I barely know Nate or his daughter anymore. Why is he trying to act like there's some strong connection between us when there isn't? He's trying to hold me to some sort of old-school, army buddy, drunken promise that they made when they were half blitzed on beer. That's a mistake. He doesn't even know the half of it. I can't promise him or anyone anything. Not now. Not ever.

"You realize things didn't quite work out that way," I say turning my head to look at him straight on. It's the first time I notice that Nate actually looks like dog shit. "I wouldn't know Ariana if I walked by her on the street."

Nate shakes his head regretfully.

"Truth be told I didn't think Jack was going to ever leave Philadelphia. Philly is in his blood. Still to this I day don't really know why he did. And then I didn't think we'd lose him so soon after that. I thought me and him had more time. Now it seems as if I don't know where the time went. You two were supposed to grow up best friends. Not strangers like this."

I don't want to talk about this shit anymore.

He's muddying the waters with this conversation.

I can't feel guilty about what I need to do.

If what Bucky says is true. Nate is a drug dealer. A heroin dealer. Just like all the others. I make no exceptions. Stealing from him will be an honor. And after I take all of his money and save my ass in the process, I'm out.

Neither he or his daughter will ever see me again.

FIVE

TINY

I sit nervously in the car and wait. Alternating between watching the police car through my rearview window and twisting my hands. I've never been stopped by the police before, and even though my father taught me numerous times what I should do if it ever happens, I'm still on edge.

A female officer gets out of the car. Immediately that makes me feel better for some reason. I guess I'm sexist. Her hair is slicked back into a neat, low ponytail and she holds her hands on her waist belt as she approaches. I roll down my window and look her in her eyes with an inquisitive but respectful "what's the problem" look.

"Ma'am, did you know that one of your rear taillights was out?"

"Oh, my goodness, no. I didn't realize that."

Oh, good this is just a courtesy stop.

"I'll get that fixed right away," I assure her.

I watch as two other officers get out of a second car that I hadn't noticed pulled up and walk directly behind her. One is a man with pale skin and bright orange hair who looks like he's fresh out of high school. The other is a tall brunette, who looks young as well, despite her stern stare and face full of acne scars.

I keep a watchful eye on them as they approach, not understanding why it takes three people to make a traffic stop, but remembering that my father taught me to stay calm and be cooperative when dealing with police officers. They're only doing their job, and I've done nothing wrong.

"May I see your driver's license, registration, and insurance card, ma'am."

"Of course."

I rifle shakily through my purse pulling out my wallet and then my license. Then I grab the registration and insurance documents for the car from behind my sun visor and hand everything over to her. I take a look at her badge. Her name is Officer Robinson. It's always good to address people by their names, so that they can better identify with you. I do that with all my patients. You'd be surprised by how many nurses don't.

"Here you go, Officer Robinson," I offer. Giving her my best smile.

The three officers return to the squad car, and the two quiet ones watch the lead officer start to run my information through what I imagine is some sort of online database. It's obvious to me now that she's showing them what to do. They must be police officer candidates or new graduates, and this is a teaching moment for them.

Fucking great.

I know that I haven't done anything wrong, but I'm still worried. There's something frightening about having to submit to people who have the authority to tell you what to do without your permission.

I consider for a moment picking up my phone and

texting my dad to tell him that I've been stopped, but then I think better of it. He's probably on the road himself, in addition to the fact that he wasn't feeling well this morning. This would just distract and worry him to death. At worst, this is probably just a matter of running my license and writing me an overpriced ticket for the taillight. At best, they'll let me go with a warning.

After about ten excruciating minutes of waiting for the officer to return, all three of them return. This time the two women are by me on the driver's side of the car, and the red-headed man is standing by the passenger side door.

"Miss Carter, did you know that your license is suspended?"

"Really...why?"

"Your license is suspended for non-payment of a moving violation."

"I am not aware of any moving violation, Officer. I'm a careful driver. I don't speed. There must be an error."

"A moving violation doesn't just mean a speeding ticket. It could be a variety of things. Driving through a stop sign. Improper turn. Driving without a seatbelt. Red light tickets. If violations like these aren't paid on time then the next step is to suspend your license which is where you're at."

Red light tickets?

Now I remember.

Fuck a duck.

A camera caught me running what I still think was a quick changing yellow light and sent a letter to my house requiring me to pay a hundred freakin' bucks. I was livid about it, and was planning on going to court to challenge it as soon as I had a day off from the hospital, but I put the ticket in my to-do pile and completely forgot about it.

Dammit.

"Can you let this go with a warning, Officer? I have an elderly father at home who's coming down with the flu. I'm a nurse and his primary caretaker. I really need to get home to him, but I promise to take care of the ticket first thing in the morning. It was an honest mistake."

I might be exaggerating about the elderly father thing a bit, my father acts younger than most men ten years younger than him, but I once saw my friend Sloan get out of a speeding ticket by pretending to cry in front of the officer. So, I know that the sympathy card works. Of course, that cop was a balding, older man of a certain age, and Sloan is a smoking hot twenty-something-year-old.

"Sorry about your father, but I'm afraid that we're going to have to charge you for driving with a suspended license."

"Really? Even though I admit that I forgot about the ticket, I honestly didn't know that my license was suspended because of it. They didn't send any notifications to my house about it."

"I'm sorry, but ignorance is not a defense."

Ugh. Maybe I would have been better off with a male cop.

"Okay, so how much is that ticket going to be then?"

I just want her to issue the ticket and get going at this point. I can tell that this woman is a stickler for the rules and only plays by the book. She's not going to budge. It's my own fault for forgetting about the ticket.

"You're being charged, Miss Carter. There is no ticket. Step out of the car please."

My stomach flip-flops.

"Wait, why?"

"I'm going to have to take you into custody."

"What do you mean into custody? Are you saying that you're arresting me?"

My heart starts to palpitate with a mixture of fear, confusion and shock. I notice that all three officers now have their hands resting on their belts. Close to their weapons. I guess I shouldn't have raised my voice, but frankly I'm stunned.

"I'm afraid not, ma'am. Now I'm going to need you to step out of the car please."

"This is unbelievable," I protest. Still not moving to exit the car. "What's going to happen to my car?" I ask when actually that's the last thing I need to be worried about. Who gives a shit about a car? I'm about to be arrested.

"It will be impounded in the municipal lot. You can get it when you're released."

Oh my God. I cannot believe this. This is straight out of a movie. A freakin' horror film. I'm being arrested for the first time in my life. Like a criminal. For a freakin' traffic ticket?!

"I just don't understand," I mutter under my breath. Nervously stuffing my phone, my sunglasses, and my Chap-Stick back into my purse. "It was just a ticket."

"I need you to get out of the car, ma'am. If I have to tell you again, I'm going to add resisting arrest to your charges."

At this point, a group of bystanders have stopped along the sidewalk and are now watching the scene unfold. I suppose it's natural for people to be curious when someone's getting arrested, especially with the national spotlight on police departments across the country, but to say that I'm completely mortified right now would be an understatement. I just pray that nobody tapes this and throws it up on YouTube.

Again, nobody's fault but my own.

And our ass backward justice system.

Don't they have real criminals to go arrest? Like the one probably already sitting in my house.

Officer Robinson asks me to hold my hands in front of me as she clasps a pair of heavy silver cuffs on my wrists. "Hold your hands together please."

They're heavier than I imagined handcuffs would feel like and they're tight. I think she put these on and tightened them not taking into account that I'm *big boned* aka on the chubby side. Maybe it's because I moved a little too slowly for her liking. Maybe because I asked too many questions. Maybe she just doesn't like her own species.

"What about my phone and my purse?"

Still asking meaningless questions. Unfortunately, I don't have a significant other to call, and luckily, I don't have a shift at the hospital tonight, but I do have one important person to answer to and he's going to be looking for me soon.

My father.

SIX

"Officer O'Reilly will grab your phone and purse for you. They'll be returned to you after you're processed at the precinct."

I sit quietly in the back of the patrol car with my legs crossed and my hands cuffed wondering what on earth I've done in a past life to deserve this night. While I get that there are way worse things that could happen to a person than being arrested for a traffic violation, for me this is way up on my list of "no way in hell" things that could ever happen to me.

I'm being arrested.

This is absolutely surreal.

I lean into the window and blow my warm breath on it. Watching little pools of condensation form. I'm not sure where we're going or even what direction we're driving in at this point. It's almost like I'm driving in a completely different city. In a completely different universe.

"Excuse me, when will I be able to make a call and let someone know what's going on?" I ask knowing that if my father gets home before me and sees that I'm not there and that I haven't called, he's going to flip.

Not because he's abnormally overprotective but because my father is a stickler for holding people accountable for doing what they say they're going to do. And we had a plan.

My father drove all day to Upstate New York to bring home an old family friend to stay with us for a while, and I'm supposed to be there to greet them upon arrival. Just the thought of meeting a convicted felon sends shivers up my spine.

Of course, I'm laughing at myself though, because isn't it ironic that my father is picking Stone up from his home of the last five years–White Pines Penitentiary, when I'm on my way to freakin' jail myself. That's going to be great dinner conversation. At least we'll have something in common.

"You can call him after you're processed."

Officer Robinson isn't being rude, but she isn't being very nice either. More like cold and indifferent. Everything can happen *after I'm processed*. What do they make a commission off of how many people they process a day? Or maybe she's tired of my questions, but that makes both of us. God knows I'm already tired of asking them.

We arrive to a police station in a neighborhood that I'm not familiar with where I'm told to sit and wait on a hard, wooden chair that wobbles. I notice that they are questioning three other women in the same main room that I'm sitting in. All three are wearing far too much makeup and far too little clothes.

A man dressed in regular clothes approaches me, but I can tell that he's a cop. Something about his walk. His approach. He must be a detective or an officer who's off duty.

"What corner did they pick you up at?" he asks in an inquisitive tone of voice.

Oh, my lord, does he think I'm a prostitute?

"I don't work any kind of corner."

"Oh...sorry." And I swear he almost laughs.

After some time passes the same man who asked me about what corner I worked on removes the cuffs from my wrists and asks me to stand over with the other women, linking us all together with what I think is called a daisy chain.

"Is this really necessary?" I ask. Feeling like their treatment of me is totally overkill. This is how they chain hardened criminals together to transport them to and from prison. Not short, curvy, nurses who run red lights.

"It's standard procedure for transport."

"Where am I going? Where's Officer Robinson?"

"It was her job to make the arrest and bring you here. Now it's my turn."

"So, I'm not being *processed* here?"

This looks like a perfectly fine precinct to me. There are four desks and a small jail cell in the corner of the room that no one is in. Why can't I stay here?

"This is just a local station. You're going to central booking where you'll be processed and then see the judge."

One of the three women, who's dressed in a very tight, red, spandex dress and wearing badly glued false eyelashes interrupts us to ask the officer a question.

"Ricky, can we make a stop before we get there?"

It doesn't get past me that she called him by his first name. Clearly, she's been arrested before. Either that or this guy is her next-door freakin' neighbor.

"Sure, Glitter. What do you want? Cheetos again?"

The officers start walking us toward a large white police

van while Ricky and Glitter continue negotiating what sounds like a planned snack stop. She asks him to grab snacks for all three of the women. Cheetos for her, Doritos for another, and a Snickers bar for the third. No one asks me what I want. Which would be to go back to sleep and start this day over again tomorrow.

I do my best to step up carefully in the van in my dress and heels, and trust me when I say that it isn't easy when you're daisy chained to a woman in front of you and in back of you. I wince slightly when the backs of my thighs touch the ice cold metal benches in the van.

"I've never seen you before. Where you do work?" The woman Glitter asks me with high suspicion in her voice.

"At Memorial Hospital," I say out loud. Hoping that both cops sitting up front will see the error of their ways. I am a normal, upstanding, law abiding citizen. *I don't belong in here* is what I really want to scream.

"Memorial Hospital? You're a square?"

"Umm, a what?"

"People with normal jobs. People who don't hustle."

"Oh well, then yeah, that's me. The square. I'm a nurse."

"What'd they arrest you for? You beat up your old man or something? Kill a patient?"

"Nothing that interesting I'm afraid. I was arrested for non-payment of a traffic ticket."

I almost topple over to one side as the officers recklessly ride over the many potholes in the streets.

"A ticket?"

"Yep."

"Seriously?"

"Seriously."

"Aww, girl, that's fucked-up."

"Sure the hell is." One of the other women agrees.

"Why'd you arrest this poor square, Ricky?"

"Wasn't me," he responds while still facing forward in the passenger seat.

"Y'all arresting squares for tickets now just to get your arrest quotas up?"

Detective Ricky turns around with a scrunched up expression across his face. Clearly not liking the insinuation my new best friend is making.

"It's because of the new quality of life laws on the books. Trying to clean up the city from the likes of you girls and your employers. You break the law and we're arresting you. Regardless of what law it is. Now if you want me and Paul to stop at the store before your long night in holding, I suggest you shut it."

Glitter completely ignores his warning.

I'm starting to really like this girl.

"That's fucked-up, Ricky. She's a nurse. Hope you never end up at her hospital on a gurney."

He glances at me briefly, but then doesn't respond to Glitter's words. I think it's pretty evident that he knows my arrest is bullshit, but he also doesn't care.

The impact of what is happening right now is starting to hit me.

Hard.

I'm handcuffed to a group of working women, hustlers, prostitutes.

I'm going to a place called central booking.

I'm going to be charged with a crime.

And I'm scared shitless.

STONE

"So where will I be sleeping?" I ask hoping that Nate hasn't made too much of a special effort to accommodate me.

"The guest room of course."

"I don't remember there being a guest room."

"It's been a while, son. Made some renovations a few years back. Stuff that Joanne always wanted me to do to the place when she was alive. I've always been good with my hands, so I put an enclosed deck off of the back of the dining room. Don't worry. It's fully insulated and heated. That's where you'll be staying."

I nod silently in approval as if it really matters where I'm sleeping. I'm not here for the accommodations. I'm here to complete a job.

"That good for you?" he asks.

"Yep," I say.

"Well just to be clear, it's not the perfect situation. There's no bathroom on the first floor, so you and Ariana will have to share hers. City was going to raise my taxes if I added another bathroom. Those assholes. But the good thing though is that Ariana cooks most nights, although she won't take any special requests no matter how much you ask. I've wanted her to fry me some trout for the longest, but she refuses to do it. Something about my cholesterol numbers."

He painfully clears his throat again.

"Nate, are you getting sick?"

"Eh...baby girl said I'm coming down with the flu and she's taking no mercy on me, because I wouldn't get that stinking flu shot last month. Thing made me sick as a dog last time I got it. Not doing that crap again no matter how much she yells at me."

We ride in silence for another few moments.

"So, you drove all the way to pick me up sick with the flu?"

"It's just a cold."

"I could have made other arrangements."

Nate turns and gives me a look as if I've insulted him.

"Your father was like a brother to me, and you just got out of the pen. Of course, I was going to pick you up. Sick or not."

I can see a layer of sheen starting to form on his forehead. He probably has a fever. I should be driving, not him, but we're stuck with him at the wheel because of my record. My license expired while I was inside, so I have to reapply and take the whole test over again in order to get it back.

"So, Stone, we need to talk about something."

"Sure."

"You realize that part of your release agreement is securing permanent employment, right?"

"Yeah."

"Any leads on something?"

"Yeah," I assure him. "I have something lined up over in Camden."

He turns his head while he continues to drive. "Camden, New Jersey?"

"Yeah," I say nonchalantly. "Keep your eyes on the road please, Nate."

Last thing I need is to have survived five years of being incarcerated only to be killed by a distracted drug dealer with the flu.

"You and I both know that you're not supposed to be leaving the state, son. The parole board won't accept a job in Jersey as legal employment."

"It's only over the bridge, and my new employer says he has a way around that technicality."

Nate tightens his face in a way that I faintly remember. The way a father would if he's annoyed but trying to be patient with a child.

"That's not going to work. If you're staying under my roof then you're going to do everything by the book."

"Don't really have the luxury of picking and choosing where I work, Nate. I'm lucky if I find anything at all. Every basic application asks if I've ever been convicted of a felony. No one wants to hire someone who's done time."

"There's one place that won't ask you that."

"I know," I say to reiterate my point. "My guy in Camden won't ask."

"There's another option." Nate coughs. "A better one. You'll work with me in the shop."

I exhale sharply. I forgot about that. Nate owns a bike shop. If there's money, I bet it's tied up some kind of way in that shop. I've got to play it cool though. Can't look too eager to get in there.

"I'm not sure if that's the best place for me."

"I'm responsible for you for however long the probationary office says I am. So, while you are under my roof, you won't be breaking any laws or any rules by working in New Jersey."

"Can you actually afford to have me working at the shop? I'm going to need a real pay stub. You can't just pay me in room and boarding."

"I've been on this earth a lot longer than you, son. I think I know what you need to show them parole officers, and I definitely know how to make money in my shop. So yeah, I will be paying you a wage. It ain't a fortune, but it'll be fair."

I wish he'd stop calling me son. He's not my de facto father. If he was, I'd like to know where the fuck he was after Jack died. I didn't hear two peeps out of him.

"You're doing too much for me. I made a big mistake, and I want to turn my life around, but I need to be the one to do it. You giving me room and board is enough."

And the Oscar goes to...

"You know, son—"

I lean my body a little bit more into the passenger side door. Damn near cringing at his use of the word son for the zillionth time today. If he says it one more time I might punch a fucking hole through the window. How easily he lets that word fly out of his mouth when I haven't seen or spoken to him for more than five minutes since Jack's funeral.

"We've only been in this car for an hour, but I'm starting to get a handle on you. I'm thinking that things have been a lot tougher on you than I ever imagined ever since Jack died."

You think, Captain Obvious?

"I'm thinking that you were about to sell them drugs, because if you didn't you were going to end up on the streets alone and afraid. But I'm also thinking that you're in the position that you're in now, because you don't know how to ask for help or graciously accept any help. That's a mistake. Real men know how to recognize a hand up and not a hand out."

I sit and stew in my own whirlpool of fury. I hate it when people think that they have me all figured out. They don't. Especially Nate. I know I've got six months to get this money, but I may not last that long if I've got to sit around and listen to this drivel all day.

Nate's cell phone rings distracting him from our conversation.

Good.

I just need for him to be quiet for ten damn minutes. Talking is overrated. One thing I learned about my life as a thief as well as my time in prison.

Silence is golden.

EIGHT

TINY

When we arrive to the building called central booking, my evening gets even crazier. I am searched, fingerprinted, and then brought into a room with two female officers who don't touch me but ask me to squat and cough while they go through my purse. They don't explain why, but I've watched enough drug documentaries to know what they're looking for. They're checking to see if I'm carrying drugs in my vagina.

It's degrading.

Demoralizing.

And frightening.

They don't even know if I'm guilty of anything yet, and they're treating me like a common criminal, yet there's nothing I can do about it. I'm under their mercy. I have to play by their rules.

It makes me think about all of the people who live on the fringes of society who this happens to on a regular basis. I feel for them. The only solace I find during this entire process is that the two officers conducting the search apologize the entire time while they're doing it. They know that this is way over the line of good policing.

After the search, Detective Ricky approaches me.

"So, Nurse Carter, I see you live near the art museum." He grins in a smarmy way. "Nice neighborhood over there."

His comment is so inappropriate on so many levels. Where's my right to privacy. And is he giving me the googly eyes?

Creepy Cop hands me off to a female officer who places me into a holding cell with the three other women I was chained to and five other women as well. There are several long wooden benches in and around the perimeter of the room, a pay phone on the wall, and a metal toilet in the corner. *There's no way I'm peeing in that thing.*

I sit on a bench in the middle of the room, and do my best to act as if I'm not frightened out of my mind. I don't think I'm fooling Glitter one bit though as she decides to talk to me about everyone in the cell.

"See that girl over there in the corner. Look at her. She's coming down. You probably see that shit all the time though, huh?"

I wasn't one hundred percent sure about that girl when I first noticed her, but Glitter confirmed it. I can tell by the size of her pupils and how agitated she is, that she seems to be coming down off of a high. Probably some sort of opioid addiction. It's an epidemic in our city.

"What'd you do to get in here, young girl?" she asks a different young woman with beautiful cocoa skin and short curly hair looking as totally out of place in here as I do.

I can't hear everything the girl is saying to Glitter, because the girl is mumbling through her tears, but I can surmise what was said based upon Glitter's responses.

"Damn, that's fucked-up. Your old man ain't shit."

She mumbles something else.

"Listen, young girl, your dude is going to save his self. Trust me when I tell you. So, you better look out for yourself. Say whatever you have to say, so that you don't get sent to Riverside. That ain't no place for a girl like you."

Glitter turns to me and reports back their conversation.

"She said she went to the store with her boyfriend to get a hoagie. Boyfriend held up the cashier while he was in there. Dummy did everything wrong. They both got pinched. She's sitting here all worried about him when she should be worried about herself. I told her that kid is going to roll on her, and she's going to end up at Riverside. I've seen it a million times."

I bet.

"Can I ask you something, Glitter?"

"Sure."

"Why do you do what you do for a living?"

"Why?" she laughs. "Because I could never do what you do. You squares give everything away for free. Your bodies, your hearts, your minds. Especially when it comes to men. When a man wants any part of me, he has to pay for the right."

What a refreshing concept. Charging someone like Bill Rappaport for an hour of my time in the sack. I should have. It was such a waste of my time I should have gotten something out of it.

After about an hour in the holding cell, I finally unclench every muscle in my body. Now that I'm relieved to see that it's highly unlikely that I'm going to be shanked, and that seeing the judge takes a really long time on a Friday night, I should probably call my house and break it to my father where I am.

Things aren't like they are on television where you get

to make the one call at a police detective's desk while he types up an arrest report. Thankfully times have changed. There's a pay phone in the cell, which any of us can use to make a call at our discretion. We just have to call collect.

This is a collect call from the Philadelphia Police Department Central Booking. Will you accept the charges?

"Yes. Hello?"

I've never been so happy to hear my father's voice in my life.

"Dad!"

"BABY GIRL!"

My father bursts into a fit of coughing. I can hear that his flu is progressing. He needs fluids, some Motrin, a pot of my chicken soup, and some sleep. I regret that I couldn't talk him out of driving upstate to pick up our new house-guest, but there was no changing his mind.

"Dad...I can't hog the phone, so let me explain what's going on. One of the taillights of my car is out. I didn't know. I was pulled over and then arrested, because my license is expired."

"That's ridiculous. I never heard of someone being arrested for a paperwork problem."

"I know, Dad, but there's some sort of new quality of life laws on the books. That's what they're calling them. I have to see the judge before I can get out of here."

"I'm coming down there."

"No, Daddy, please. You sound awful. I don't want you running around in this damp weather with a fever. Plus, there's nothing you can do. Glitter told me that the longest part of this whole ordeal is that they have to run my finger-prints through the system in Harrisburg, and that it's going to take a long time because I don't have a record. But once that's done I'll see the judge and be released."

"Who the heck is Glitter?"
"One of my cellmates."
"Is she a whore?!"
"Shhh...yes, Dad."
Silence
"Flu or no flu, I'll be there in under twenty minutes."

NINE

STONE

"You think I'm going to let you break the law two seconds fresh out of prison?"

"I have a driver's license on me, Nate."

"An expired one."

"Not going to argue about this."

"Even if I order you not do it?"

"Don't take orders anymore. Even from you. I'm fine and you're getting sicker by the minute. You're pulling over and I'm driving us the rest of the way."

"I wouldn't be able to live with myself if we get stopped, son."

"Did Ariana sound okay to you?"

His head eyes drop.

"She was trying to be strong, but no. I know my daughter. She's never been in trouble a day in her life. She's scared."

"Then I think it's safe to say that we have extenuating circumstances. She's not okay. You're not okay. And I'm fine to drive."

"Nobody's going to care that my daughter was just

released from prison and that I've got the flu if we get stopped."

"I didn't know you were such a law abiding citizen."

"You become a lot of things when you get old, son. I used to take a lot of risks. Now I play by the rules. It's just easier that way."

Interesting choice of words. Too bad they're all starting to sound like he has a mouth of marbles.

"Well, I'll risk it. Pull over. Your throat sounds like it's closing up on you."

"Fine," he huffs. "You can drive, but first thing tomorrow you're going to see about applying for a new driver's license."

"Uh-huh."

"First thing, Stone."

"Understood."

The last thing I feel like doing after getting out of my five year cage is running right back into another one, but Ariana is going to be released soon and Nate is sick as a dog. Me doing this will probably go a long way in gaining Nate's trust. Slow and steady wins the race.

"I'm going to pull an up-to-date picture of her on my phone. Just so you know who to look for when you get inside the building."

"I'm going to have to wait for her outside."

"Why?"

"You need a valid state ID to enter a police building like central booking."

"Oh, yeah right. I didn't think of that. Let's agree that you can drive to the house and drop yourself off, but I'm going to need to go get her myself. Just in case she's going to be longer than we think. I can go inside."

"Fine."

We pull over on the shoulder of the turnpike. After we

switch sides, Nate hands me his phone with his photo app open.

"Take a look at her anyway. This picture was taken two months ago."

Nate bursts into a coughing fit.

"Adjust the seat back, Nate, and take a nap. I'll use your navigation to get us to your house."

"I'll lie back, but I'm not going to be able to sleep. Too wound up."

"Just try and catch some z's at least. I'm not pulling off until you lean back."

"Just like your father. So damn combative. Wait a minute before you pull off. I've never had to put my own passenger seat back before. Let me just find the lever."

While Nate spends the next few minutes trying to figure out how to adjust his seat, I click on one of the pictures on his phone of Ariana, and I almost shit my pants.

She's dressed in a sea blue colored dress. The kind of dress that has one sleeve and leaves her other arm bare. You can tell it's a dress that isn't meant to be purposely provocative. It's tasteful. Kind of expensive. It doesn't display any great amount of cleavage or slit up the leg. But it doesn't have to. The way the dress skims along the curves of Ariana's body is damn near pornographic.

Breasts that sit high.

An ass that looks so round and firm that I could bounce a quarter off of it.

A small waist that makes both those breasts and ass look even more pronounced and mouthwatering.

A smile that could stop traffic.

Sultry umber colored eyes that are so expressive that they seem as if they are searing straight into my soul through the photograph.

This is *not* the little dork with a towel tied around her neck pretending to save the world like a Powerpuff Girl in her bedroom anymore.

This picture is of a grown-ass woman who I'd pay to see with that tiny pink Powerpuff Girl towel wrapped around her curvaceous body. And the only thing she'd need to be worried about saving was her sweet curvy ass from the likes of me.

I'm so transfixed by the picture that I don't notice at first that Nate has finished adjusting his seat and is staring curiously at me.

"You ready?" he asks.

Hell no, I think to myself.

I'm not even close to being ready.

I'm nowhere ready to live in the same house as the woman in this photograph for one day much less six fucking months.

TEN

TINY

My time in front of the judge is about the only thing that's happening quickly tonight. The judge seems to be pushing through his pile of cases in record breaking speed.

"Who's next?" he asks his clerk.

My public defender is a young woman who seems to care quite deeply about women's rights, and seems utterly outraged by my arrest.

"This is ridiculous." She leans over and speaks quietly in my ear. "Do you want me to fight this or do you want to plead and pay the ticket."

"Will it be on my permanent record if I plead? I just want to get this over with."

She shuffles a couple of papers in her hand then speaks again.

"If you plead guilty, I could probably get it expunged. In fact, I know I can."

"Okay, then I'll take a plea."

"Are you sure? Because this arrest was a colossal waste of everyone's time and taxpayer's money."

I know. I know. I should probably fight this whole thing, but I just don't have the energy. I want to get out of here, climb into my bed, and forget this whole day ever happened.

"I'm sure. I'll take the plea."

I sign about a thousand pieces of paper including one to agree to the deal and one to get my belongings out of lock up. When I exit the building, tears of relief flood my eyes. It's been a long night and according to Glitter, I was lucky to get out of there when I did.

"Some squares have to stay locked up all weekend, because they don't have any prints in Harrisburg. Takes them longer to process."

None of the arresting officers gave me a second to turn off my phone when it was confiscated, so now it's dead. There's no way for me to call my father to see if he made it back to Philly yet. I just hope and pray that he's made it here already. I won't be able to drive my own car.

The court was on the second floor, so as I make my way down to the main floor, I barely place my foot down on the third step when I hear my father's weakened voice.

"Baby girl."

"Dad!"

I run into his arms like I did when he picked me up from overnight Girl Scout camp the first and last year I ever attended. He holds me tight then grabs me at the shoulders and moves me back so he can look at me.

"You okay?"

"Yes, just tired."

"They let you off?"

"I had a public defender, and I plead guilty to the charge."

He makes a face. I can tell he's disappointed in my decision. My father is a big believer in fighting for what's right, so he probably wanted me to challenge the charges.

"I'm sorry, Dad, but a hot shower and a half decent toilet were calling me. I didn't realize how dependent I am on the creature comforts of life. Like privacy and running water and not having to eat bologna sandwiches."

I kiss his cheek.

"You ate a bologna sandwich?" He chuckles.

"Absolutely not. Luckily for me I just had dinner out before my arrest. So, I skipped the sandwich."

"Whores and bologna." He shakes his head in disgust. "Jail is no place for you, baby girl. You're my little princess. This is definitely not a place that I ever thought you'd see the inside of."

"I wasn't in Alcatraz. It was literally just four hours of my life spent with some prostitutes and drug addicts. Relax." I smile. Trying to put him at ease even though it was actually the scariest four hours I think I've ever spent. Not because of the women I was in there with (because a few of them weren't that bad), but simply because I didn't like the feeling of being powerless and waiting for the unknown.

"Joanne is probably turning over in her grave."

"You cremated Mom," I deadpan.

"You know what I mean."

My dad tries to hold back a couple more deep coughs, but I can hear the mucus rumbling around in his chest and his skin looks sallow.

"You don't look so good. Let's get you home."

"Yeah, I'm a little tired. I parked over there, hun. Maybe you should drive."

Now I know he's sick. He never lets me drive the Chevy.

"Where's your car by the way?" he asks.

"They put it in some police impound lot that's five miles away. It's closed now, so I'll have to come back and get it tomorrow."

"What a pain in the ass. Do you have to work tomorrow?"

"Nope."

"Good. So, once you pick it up tomorrow, bring it by the shop. I can get one of the techs to fix the light. In fact, I'm going to have them give that car a thorough work up. Not sure how I missed your taillight being out."

I interlock my arm with my father's as we walk side by side to the truck.

"You're not responsible for everything, Dad. You're my superman, but you're not *the* superman."

"When did you find me out?" he jokes.

"So, where's this infamous son of Jack at? Why didn't he come with you?"

He smiles. "I dropped him off at the mall on my way here. The boy needed some toiletries, fresh underwear, and things like that. Had to twist his arm though. He doesn't like to accept help. I can tell it's going to take him some time getting used to kindness. Probably hasn't seen that in a very long time."

Probably not, I think. Even I have to admit that if I had to endure five years of what I just did for four hours, I would be crawling up the freakin' walls.

"Do you think he's dangerous?"

"Anyone has the capability of violence, baby girl."

"I'm not talking in abstracts. I'm asking you if he did time in prison for more than drugs. Five years is a long time for just possession."

"What do you know about any of that?" he asks somewhat visibly shaken. Sometimes he treats me like I'm still a naïve teenager.

"I watch the news, Dad."

"Drug laws are often enforced arbitrarily and vary from state to state. I don't know the details about Stone's case, and honestly, I don't need to know. It's over and he's home. That's all that matters."

Home? This isn't his home.

"Correction, that's all that matters to you. I just spent four hours of my life in a cell with eight lightweight criminals. So, excuse me if I'm not so keen on sharing my house with a potentially dangerous one."

ELEVEN

TINY

As soon as we get home, I practically shove two Motrin down my dad's throat and order him to get into bed. Then I make a beeline for the bathroom.

I take the longest pee ever. You know how when you hold your urine too long and then when you finally go it takes forever to trickle out? That was me. Next up was a shower. I felt gross. After a long day at work, dinner, and an arrest by Philadelphia's finest—I was more than ready to wash the day away and binge watch a Netflix series.

I'm sitting on the couch with my legs bent underneath me and a pint of pistachio ice cream in hand when Bottle runs toward the front door, hearing a stranger's car pull up way before I do. Bottle is my chocolate brown, seventy-five pound, rescue Labrador retriever named after her number one obsession. Crushing plastic water bottles with her jaws.

"Who is it, Bottle?" I ask her in my soft, baby-like voice. "Is it the guy who's going to smother us in our sleep tonight?"

I have to laugh at myself. Maybe I'm being too hard on this son of Jack. Maybe he has some redeeming qualities.

Bottle's tail wags and she begins jumping up and down. Circling around and around in front of the door. Excited that someone is coming to visit. Actually, a little too excited. Neither of us have ever been really good about training her not to jump on people or furniture.

I stand on my tiptoes, and peek through the door's small glass window pane. I want to get a glimpse of him before he comes inside.

Stone.

What kind of a name is that? I think my dad mentioned once that he's had that name ever since he can remember. Did Jack name him that when he adopted him? Or was that his name before. I mean who nicknames a kid Stone? Only a parent who thinks that their child is destined for a life of crime or maybe a boxer or even a rapper. Definitely not your average term of endearment.

Bottle starts scratching at the door as I watch a silver Honda with an Uber sticker in the window come to a complete stop in front of our driveway. I reprimand her for jumping, mostly because my anxiety is feeding off of her frenetic energy.

"Shh, Bottle. Sit!"

It's dark out and the glare from the glow of the light post prevents me from clearly seeing Stone's face while he's still seated in the car; but when one of the back doors open and a large booted foot lands heavily on the concrete, I inhale a quick breath.

He's definitely no longer the boy I remember from an old picture my father has of him in one of our family photo albums. The young boy in a transformers T-shirt with a permanent scowl etched across his face.

That boy is gone and has morphed into a man.

A mammoth of a man.

When he completely exits the car he literally takes my breath away.

He's tall.

He's got to be at least three or four inches over six feet tall.

And he's wide.

Like a Mack truck.

He looks like he could swallow me whole.

Sheesh, maybe they sprinkle their food with Miracle Gro in prison.

Bottle can no longer contain herself as she starts barking as he begins walking toward the front door. She's very excited about the new human entering her domain. Bottle loves people. Other dogs not so much.

The unexpected noise of her bark startles Stone, and he glances toward the window. When he does I move quickly away from it like the weirdo that I am. Obviously I don't want him knowing that I'm peeping through the window like a creeper. I'm not sure whether or not he saw me. I didn't see any sort of look of recognition pass across his face.

"Quiet, girl."

I shush my dog and run into the kitchen, pretending like I'm working on my dad's soup which is actually already finished. I knew he had already dozed off after my shower, so I was going to wait to bring it to him later.

The doorbell rings.

Damn, didn't Dad give him a key?

"Baby girl, I think that's Stone," my father calls out.

"I thought you were asleep," I fuss back.

"Can't sleep until the house is settled."

My heart is racing and I feel jittery. I take a quick look at my reflection in the refrigerator, smooth a bit of my curls behind my ear, and then the realization hits me. My anxiety is not based in fear, but because I'm actually nervous. Nervous about what this strange felon is going to think about me.

Will he remember me?

Will he think that I'm pretty?

Am I losing my damn mind?

The bell rings again.

Oh crap, now I hear my father around.

"Never mind, Ariana. I'll get the door," he says grumbling. "You're always so slow."

Yeah, slowly losing my common sense.

He beats me to the door, so I just stay in the kitchen. Suspended in motion. Using a wooden spoon to stir a pot of my homemade chicken and rice soup that's already finished cooking.

I can hear the two of them clunking around the living room moving toward the enclosed deck. Carrying what I suspect are Stone's purchases to his new abode. Dad has spent the last seventy-two hours getting what was once a neglected pet project of his into an actual livable space for Stone. It looks really nice now.

He installed insulation and drywall and painted it a soft sugar cookie batter color (my paint selection). He also bought a dark brown sofa bed on clearance, which will be great if Bottle decides to lay on it, because you won't be able to see her hair on the couch at first glance (another one of my bright ideas). Vacuuming Bottle's fur is definitely one of my least favorite chores to do. Pretending that it's not there because it blends in with the couch is a much better plan.

"Sit, girl!" I hear my father reprimand Bottle. I can hear her claws clicking and sliding across the floor. She's definitely jumping all over the place.

"Sorry, Stone." I hear him apologize. "She's just excited."

While my dad has never said the words, I think that he is the one who's beyond excited that his dear deceased friend's son is coming to live with us. My father loves to live his life swaddled in the memories of the people he loved. Jack included.

"What's taking you so long, baby girl?" he asks from the other room. I can hear him settling into his recliner. An ugly piece of furniture that he refuses to donate or toss or preferably burn.

"I'm fixing your soup."

"Smells good but give it a rest, and come out here to say hi to Stone."

I plunk the wooden spoon down on the counter and take a deep cleansing breath as I wipe my clammy hands on a dish towel.

"Coming."

I'm being silly. If my friends Sloan and Elizabeth could see me they would smack me into next week. I give myself an inner tongue lashing in honor of their absence.

I take a final breath and walk into the living room with a wide smile and my boobs pointed high.

He's just another man.

His opinion doesn't matter.

Let me just get this introduction over with.

TWELVE

TINY

I make a memorable entrance just as I feared I would.

Slipping and falling straight to the floor.

I polished the wood floors two days ago with the wrong cleaning product making the floors slippery as an oil slick. That's why Bottle is slipping all over the place, and that's exactly why I too fall straight on my ass.

Landing right on my tailbone, I feel a sharp pain that shoots up my spine and makes me want to burst out in tears. Not just because of the pain of the fall, but because it's simply icing on the cake of a shitty day.

"Shit!" I exclaim.

When I look up from the ground, I realize that I've fallen down in front of the most spectacular man I've ever seen in my life.

Stone looks like every bad boy fantasy I've ever had since I was fourteen years old. Even dressed in a burgundy colored hoodie that looks like it's two sizes too small for his sinewy body—he looks delicious. Delicious in the most imperfect way you can imagine.

Slightly bowed but muscular legs.

A strong but crooked jaw.

Crooked nose.

Piercing gray eyes.

Upon first sight, it seems that most parts of him are covered in rough edges, scars, and hard lines, yet my gut tells me that there's something much softer inside. Something deep buried underneath a lot of coarse layers. A vulnerability that he's probably never revealed to anyone. I don't know exactly how I know that. I just know that I do.

"Hey," he says with a basically unreadable expression. "You all right?"

He shoves one of his sleeves up and then offers me his hand. I've never seen a sexier forearm in my life. Muscular and strong and covered in ink and prominent veins fighting for their place under his skin.

"Hi." Is my simple response. Doing my best to close my mouth as I accept his help off the floor.

"Not sure if you remember, Stone, but baby girl can be a little accident prone."

"Dad—"

"But she's a great cook. That more than makes up for it."

It's a simple thing, but it doesn't escape me how he doesn't have to exert an ounce of energy to pull me off of the floor. He just does it with virtual ease.

"So how was the ride down?" I ask Stone as I wait patiently for some of my dignity to reemerge.

"Uneventful," Stone answers and he looks as if it pained him to utter even that single word. I'm thinking that small talk is not his thing.

"Hey, I'm starving!" My dad interjects. Coughing only seconds later. "How about you go wash your hands and get ready for the chicken soup, Stone. Smells damn good doesn't it. She makes it with wild rice instead of noodles just like Jo used to make. It's going to fix me right up."

Stone gives my father a quiet nod in agreement, then he turns his head around as if he's looking for something.

"The restroom is upstairs right next to Ariana's room," my father says. Making an educated guess at what Stone was looking for. Beats me how he figured that out. I have zero idea what's going on behind those piercing cold eyes of his and that flat affect.

Yeah, he's going to kill us in our sleep.

"Go show Stone where it is, baby girl, and I'll keep an eye on the pot."

"Just don't eat it yet," I warn my father. "There's a way I like to serve it."

"Then make sure you hurry up." He chuckles. "Mmm, it smells almost as good as your mom's. Can't wait to taste it."

I start walking toward the stairway and can feel my heart literally trying to pound its way through my breast-bone. Beating in tandem with each step I take.

Up left. Up right.

Up left. Up right.

Stone is keeping pace directly behind me, and I feel super self-conscious about it. I don't like for people to walk directly behind me. Especially men. Mainly because I'm not a small girl. There's nothing petite about me. Hence the nickname, Tiny. An obvious play on words. Even my fingers are the sizes of Vienna sausages thanks to some sort of reces-sive trait that my maternal great-grandmother passed on to me.

It definitely doesn't help that I'm wearing my weekend leggings. You know the pair. Not the ones with enough firm spandex to suck you in all the right places, but rather the super comfy pair that you wear around the house to watch

TV in. The pair I have on right now are boring, blue, cotton ones that I picked up from Walmart on clearance. They do absolutely nothing for my butt, but they sure feel good when I'm binge watching *Supernatural*.

Stone doesn't say a word as he follows me up the stairwell. He's either transfixed or grossed out by the gelatin-like jiggle of my butt cheeks. I must admit that they can be a startling sight. Sometimes I catch a glimpse of my ass in the mirror when I'm getting dressed in the morning and wonder when did all of "that" jiggle happen to me. It just kind of appeared out of nowhere. Or maybe years of eating brownies and vanilla ice cream for dessert have something to do with it.

As I move closer to the top of the second floor, the quiet between us becomes so unsettling, that I feel the need to fill the empty space with words.

"Do you remember visiting here as a kid?"

I realize how stupid the question is after it flies out of my mouth, but I didn't know what else to say, so I wait patiently for his response. Dying for him to talk to me about anything at this point. Distracting him from my gelatin butt.

"I remember."

"I kind of remember too. I think our parents made you babysit me a couple of times. What are you four or five years older than me?"

That was dumb to say too. Do I really want to remind him of the nerdy kid I used to be? No, I want him to see me as the woman that I am today. Smart. Accomplished. A good daughter. Actually, scratch all of that.

He's been in jail for five years. Who am I trying to impress? Plus, I'm sure that Stone doesn't give two craps about anything right now except for a hot meal and a warm bed. Hell, I was in jail for four hours and that's all I seem to want. I'm sure he has a lot more things on his mind that are way more important. Struggles that I can't even fathom.

"So here it is," I say stopping in front of the bathroom. "I left a clean towel and washcloth for you on the counter. I'm pretty much a neat freak, so don't worry about having to clean or anything," I say babbling like an imbecile. "And I'm sorry about the flower wallpaper in here. Maybe Dad can change it to something more neutral when he gets a chance."

Stone stares at me with the oddest look on his face. If I had to guess, I'd say it's a cross between wanting to puke and wanting to shake me senseless.

"There's nothing that you need to apologize to me about."

"I'm sorry—"

"I asked you to stop apologizing." His voice grows deeper and firmer.

I clamp my mouth shut, because I swear I was just about to apologize for apologizing.

"I need to go check on my soup. You come down when you're ready," I say and then head full speed ahead down the steps. I think I even skipped a couple of steps trying to get away from him as fast as I could.

He watches me as I scamper away. Probably trying to make sure I don't fall flat on my behind again. When I reach the bottom of the stairs, Bottle is patiently waiting for me with a sloppy lick on the back of my hand. This gesture only assures me that I must be a complete basket case. Bottle only licks me calmly when I'm the one who's anxious or angry. She has a knack for always sensing my energy. She should have been a therapy dog.

I wasn't expecting this.

But something about this guy makes me step back in a

virtual time machine and become a total dweeb again. I look like a straight-up amateur. Like I've never had a conversation with a hot as sin man before. Like he can smell the "virgin" on me.

It's bad enough that I didn't even want him here and what has started out as a sucky day has now officially turned into the worst day ever.

Of course, it doesn't take Nathaniel Carter aka *Columbo* long to take notice.

THIRTEEN

TINY

"What's wrong?" My father asks with a fair amount of concern.

"Nothing."

"Did he say something to you?"

Always my superman.

"No, Dad."

"I know you were never a hundred percent on board with this plan, hun, but give Stone some time. Life has dealt him a shitty hand."

"You've made that abundantly clear the hundreds of times we discussed this."

"Your mother always opened the house to friends and family in need. It's the Christian thing to do."

"You haven't been to church in twenty years. Now stop talking. It isn't good for your throat."

I put my hand on his forehead to check his temperature.

"Of course, if he gets out of pocket, let me know. You know I don't play that mess."

"Calm yourself, Rambo. He's fine. It's just...I don't know what to say to him. I'm saying all the wrong things."

He relaxes his face.

"Oh, is that all? Just be yourself, baby girl. That's all you can do. I bet he'll be in a much better mood after he eats some of your cooking. I swear it smells just like your mom's soup. You get closer and closer to her secret recipe every time you make it."

I do my best to smile in response to my father, but it's getting more difficult, not easier, as the years go by without Mom. I know he genuinely meant what he said about the soup as a compliment, but it doesn't feel that way. It feels like a backhanded compliment. Like I'm not doing a good enough job filling her shoes.

In fact, I'm pretty sure that I'm doing a really piss-poor job of filling my mother's shoes. Probably because I don't want to fill them. I shouldn't have to. I'm not his wife. I'm his daughter and her death has left me with my own hollow parts to fill. Her passing was senseless, painful, and I'm never going to accept it.

Unlike my mom, I'm serving the chicken soup with a few fresh herbs on top as a garnish and warm rosemary olive oil bread in the same way I've seen some of the chefs do on the Food Network.

Stone finally returns from the second floor and stops at the entrance of the kitchen and watches me silently. I'm starting to think that he likes to observe. Like I'm an animal in the zoo. A very odd and clumsy animal.

I turn to see what he wants, but his intense glare almost causes me to drop one of my mother's handmade ceramic bowls on the floor. His eyes are the color of a full moon.

"You need help?" he asks. Shocking the shit out of me. I didn't expect him to be...helpful.

I shake my head no. "Uh-uh."

He ignores my response and starts opening up cabinets

anyway. He finds and grabs three spoons and drinking glasses. Making sure to rinse and wipe each of them down with a clean paper towel.

"Stone didn't eat much on the way here, so make sure to fill his bowl," my father calls out from the den.

"I don't eat much," Stone says with a curtness. "Don't fill it."

And oh hell, I swear his voice just dropped about ten octaves when he gave that almost angry order. Stone has a very deep, rich, and distinctive voice. In a crowd of ten thousand men, I could pick him out. It's a sumptuous and heavy voice, and any other day I'd be turned on by it, but not right now.

Right now, I'm trying to understand why he sounds so indignant, and he's literally only been in our house for ten damn minutes. What the hell did we do to him? I know he's been through a lot but *sheesh.*

"Then don't eat," I say with a bit of edge to my voice.

I don't even have to see him; I can feel my father reprimanding me from the other room.

"Or maybe just eat a little bit," I say trying to clean things up. I make sure to keep my back toward him. "I'll go grocery shopping after I liberate my car tomorrow and get you some of the things you like, if that would be better for you. Just make a list."

"Liberate your car?"

"The police impounded it after I was arrested."

"What kind of car."

"An old BMW wagon."

It was my mothers.

"You drive a station wagon?"

I feel a lot of judgment in the air from someone who probably hasn't driven in five damn years.

"I'm sorry but what exactly are you driving?"

His mouth stays firmly shut but his eyes.

They're rippling.

Like molten silver.

"I don't need anything special from the store," he says with a clipped voice. "Whatever you cook is fine. Where are the napkins?"

Jackass.

"I've got 'em," I say dismissively. "Just get out of my kitchen and go sit down."

FOURTEEN

TINY

This is torture.

The three of us sit quietly at the dining room table and eat our meals while we catch up on sports news on ESPN. Actually, the two of them catch up on sports. I on the other hand start to push my spoon back and forth in my bowl and reminisce about the last time my mom made soup for us.

It was the summer before the accident. I was sick with mono and feeling lethargic and depressed. I wanted to be outside with my friends, but I just didn't have the energy. So, she made a pot of this soup as her surefire way of curing me from the inside out. My mom believed that food was the best medicine, but her soup damn sure didn't taste this salty. It makes me want to throw my bowl against the wall.

God, I suck at this.

"So, how's work?" my father asks. Looking at me with gentle eyes as if he knows what I'm feeling, but obviously there's no way that he could. He's slurping the soup like it's the best thing he's ever eaten. I bet the salt has to be burning his raw throat.

"It's good. You know I love my shifts in the emergency room."

And I do. I love being an ER nurse. The shifts are grueling, but the work is meaningful. I get to treat people when they're at their most vulnerable. When they're most frightened. People need a firm hand yet an empathetic heart when they come into the ER, and I think I've mastered the art of how to administer both.

"What's to love about treating people with the flu during the week and gunshot victims over the weekend."

I roll my eyes. We've been over this ad nauseam. While I know that my father is proud of me, he's always been vocal about the fact that he'd rather I work in the bike shop with him than as a nurse. He thinks I'm in constant danger, and the protective part of his personality can't stand it.

"Gunshot victims go to the hospital across town, Dad. They have a better triage for those types of injuries. I've been telling you that for years. And what hospital do you think I'm going to work in that doesn't have its share of people with the flu? If you don't get some sleep soon, you're probably going to be the next patient I admit."

I'm not totally sure, but I think I see the tiniest smirk form on Stone's face. Wait, nope. He was just belching.

"So, you actually like working around sick people all day?"

"Yes, Dad." I exhale with aggravation. "I love my job. I've told you this about a thousand times."

I check my cell phone after it makes a series of beeps and also some vibrations. All different notifications for incoming emails and texts I missed while my phone was dead.

Stone gives my phone a curious look. I'm not sure why. I

know he's been incarcerated for a while, but I don't think cell phones have evolved that much over the last five years.

"Well, while Florence Nightingale here works weird hours, you will be starting at ten a.m. every day," my father says to Stone. "We're going to need to leave the house about nine to open on time."

"You're not going to work, Daddy," I say waving my hand dismissively.

"And you're going to be working at the shop?" I ask Stone.

He looks at my father first before answering and so do I. My dad is crazy if he thinks I'm going to let him go to work with the flu, plus he never mentioned anything about Stone working at the shop. Living with us and working in the family business? That's quite a lot of access for someone we don't really even know.

"Yeah," Stone responds somewhat indifferently.

I guess someone isn't too thrilled about his new job. Well how about that. That makes two of us.

"Are you finished eating, Dad?"

I walk around and lift his bowl off of the table before waiting for an answer.

"Uh oh," he says. "Guess I'm in trouble. She swiped my dinner."

"No trouble," I say. Doing my best to lie. "You're finished with your soup and I think you should get to bed. You have a fever."

"All right, hun. I know you're probably exhausted from your day. Thanks for the meal."

After my dad goes to bed, I quietly begin clearing the dishes while Stone basically stares at the last spoonfuls of soup in his bowl. I lean over to clear his bowl, but he holds it down with both of his hands so that I can't lift it.

"Leave it," he says tersely.

Both of Bottle's ears perk up and she sits on her hind legs staring very carefully at Stone. She doesn't like his energy and frankly neither do I.

"I thought you were finished."

"I am."

"Then let me take the damn bowl," I say with an attitude.

He continues to grip the bowl and raises his eyes to meet mine.

"I'll do it."

Bottle growls lowly at Stone. At least somebody in this house has my back.

"I want to clean the kitchen before I go to bed so–"

"You don't want me here, do you?"

I give deep consideration to what I'm going to say in response to Stone's very straightforward question. My father and I spent fourteen long days arguing about how much "help" he was going to give to Stone after his release.

I thought that my father's generosity should have ended with giving him a small starter loan and the occasional listening ear if things were tough at first. My father disagreed. He wanted to do more.

So, when Stone called and asked if he could stay indefinitely at our house, my father jumped at the chance to say yes. It was exactly the type of big gesture he was looking for. He was ecstatic about it. Me not so much.

But Stone seems to be a straight shooter aka asshole, so there's no need to handle him with kid gloves. Direct is best with a guy like this.

"No, I don't want you here."

And then the oddest thing happens after that.

He smiles.

STONE

I'm an early riser.

Five years of waking up when correctional officers tell you to will do that. I spend the first thirty minutes or so of my day working out: push-ups, planks, crunches a few simple stretches. It clears my head for whatever bullshit I'm going to have to put up with for the rest of the day and gets me focused.

I'm finishing up a set when Nate knocks on my door, fully dressed, and ready to escort me to my first day of work.

"Ariana is still sleeping, so we need to get moving before she wakes up to walk Bottle."

"Because you don't want her finding out that you're out of bed?"

"She's making a big deal out of a little cold."

"You look like crap, Nate."

I need him to stay home, and I certainly don't need him thinking that he has to take me to work every day. I'm never going to be able to get access to his files if he's there watching me like a hawk.

"I feel like crap, but that's not the point. When you own

a business, you have to run it. I have to go in for at least a half an hour today and make sure everything is all right in there. If I don't, I won't be able to relax."

This man seems to carry a lot of anxiety. That's where I can probably be of assistance. If I can figure out what he's most worried about, what would relieve some of his angst, I could lock this whole job up in under six months. It's simple. Identify the problem, insert myself as the solution, then take advantage of the situation.

"Let me grab a shower, and I'll be ready in fifteen."

I climb the stairs quietly with my new bag of toiletries and briefly glance at Ariana's closed door. I can't help but smile to myself. I had a dream last night. A funny one. Ariana poured a bowl of chicken and wild rice soup over my head. Then I made her lick it all off.

I like Ariana, and I like that she doesn't like me.

That means she's tough.

She's also sexy.

And definitely smart.

Maybe a little too smart.

I'm going to have to be really careful that she doesn't catch on to my real agenda here, because it's for damn sure that she's paying attention.

SIXTEEN

STONE

I'm standing in Nate's hot-ass bike shop, leaning against the front counter with my arms crossed, defenses high, listening to his tough guy lecture between short bouts of his feverish coughing.

"I've got three rules if this shit is going to work. Number one is that I pay salaries with a paycheck, and I pay commissions with cash under the table. Your salary isn't going to be shit, but it will give you the pay stub you need, plus your commissions should be decent enough if you can sell bikes. It's not rocket science. Harleys sell themselves."

I've learned a couple of interesting things about my new boss this morning. First is that Nate owns the largest and oldest bike shop specializing in sales and repairs of Harley Davidson's in Philadelphia. It's damn near a neighborhood treasure, and has been standing in the same location since his grandfather opened it in the early 1980s. A great place to wash drug money.

Second is that he takes his business very seriously. I can't fuck around in here. I'm going to have to be very strategic about what I say and do.

Third is that Nate talks and acts *very* differently when he's not around his daughter. He's harder, tougher, and uses way more profanity. The kind of man I remembered was my father's best friend.

It's kind of funny. Without me having to work him at all, he's just revealed to me his number one weakness...Ariana. He's different with her. Softer with her. She is his weak spot, but I totally understand the reason why.

He knows that his daughter is something special.

The total package.

Curvy as fuck, sexy as hell, smart as a whip, sweet as pie (all right maybe not that sweet), but she can cook her ass off. So there's that.

Any father in his right mind would be overprotective of her. God knows what Nate would do if he had any idea that I've been thinking about her perfectly round ass jiggling up those stairs ever since I woke up with a bad case of morning wood.

Not to mention my shower this morning. I relieved myself of a lot of pent up aggression as I came all over those shower tiles. It was the way she spoke to me last night. That heart shaped mouth. Those smart-ass words flying out of it. Plus, the fact that I knew she was only a few steps away from me. Lying in her bed right on the other side of the wall. Just the thought had me releasing myself under the hot streams of water pounding down my back.

Fuck, it felt good.

But God knows what *she* would do if she knew that was going on right on the other side of her bedroom wall, because it's obvious that Ariana Carter doesn't like me even a little bit.

That's good though. She needs to keep disliking me. It will keep her out of danger. I don't know if Bucky has eyes on me or not, but I imagine he does. So, I don't even want him catching me and Ariana breathing the same air, or he might decide to put plan B into action right away. Something tells me that he would get greater satisfaction at watching me break Nate's daughter than getting his seven million dollars back. I wonder what the fuck Nate took from him?

"Number two is that I don't pay for health insurance. You'll need to buy that on your own, or have Ariana check you out once a year. Hell, baby girl probably knows more than most doctors anyway."

A brief but dirty thought runs through my head.

Ariana and I playing doctor.

Damn, I need to get some ass...and soon.

"And number three...don't touch Savannah."

Savannah is Nate's only full-time employee. She seems to be a jack of all trades. She does some paperwork, orders supplies, answers phones, but mostly she sells bikes. And I see why. She's hot as fuck. In a 1940s, tattooed, pin-up model kind of way.

She's wearing a black tank with the Carter Bike logo on it, a pair of cut off jean shorts, black Doc Martens, and her hair in some sort of pin curls with a folded red bandana tied around them. She has the perfect look for the shop. A biker's dream. Her major flaw though is that she's outside having a morning smoke. Everyone has their vices, but for me, women who smoke are a huge turnoff. So, Nate doesn't have to worry about me. I'm not interested.

"You sure you don't need me in repairs?" I ask Nate. "I work best with my hands. Did a lot of that while I was inside. Having me try to sell on the showroom floor is probably the worst place for someone like me."

"I only have licensed techs back there. You'd need to

train and get your license like everyone else if you want to be a mechanic. Until such time, the only place I can put you is on the floor."

I shake my head in disagreement. Hoping to convince him otherwise.

"That's not where I'm going to be the most effective."

I need to get in the back and make friends with the technicians. They're the ones who probably know where all the bodies are buried. My gut tells me that even though Savannah handles sales, she doesn't know shit. She knows what Nate wants her to know.

"Do you want to go back inside of those four walls and finish serving the remainder of your sentence?"

"No."

"Then why are we still talking about this? You'll learn a lot from selling the bikes."

"Understood."

He turns his back to me when I decide to speak again.

"Why are you doing all of this for me, Nate?"

"Why?" He takes a chug of some orange juice.

"Yeah, why."

"You're Jack's son and he didn't raise no idiot. You just need help getting back on your feet again and I'm just the man to do it. That's why."

I have to ask this.

The question has been burning a hole in my tongue for twenty-four hours.

"So where was all that help a few years ago?"

Nate's eyes grow slightly wider. Evidently surprised by my frankness.

"I haven't asked you anything about why you aren't living in Jack's house anymore. About where all of his life insurance money went. His truck. His gun collection. You know why? Because I understand that shit happens. You should understand that too."

"You saying that you dropped the ball because shit happens?"

"I'm saying that I didn't have no ball to drop. It wasn't my job to raise you right. That was Jack's job. I assumed he completed that job. When he died, you were already eighteen years old. Not eight. When I was eighteen I was already serving in the army, paying my grandmother's bills, and defending this country. Don't blame me for your bad decisions."

He's defensive, coughing like crazy, and in an all-around bad mood now. I shouldn't have said what I did. Having this conversation about would've, should've, could've shit is not going to help my cause right now. I sound like an ungrateful dickhead, and that isn't going to get Nate to trust me. That's not going to help me get my money.

"You're right," I say respectfully. "I won't bring it up again. So, what are the hours I'll be working again?"

"I need someone to work late in the shop when Savannah's here. That's why I really need you out front and not in the back. She works nights and most weekends, but it's not safe for her to be in here on her own anymore. Her mother and I are old high school friends, and she would kill me if something were to happen to Savannah."

Oh, so that's why he wants me to keep my hands to myself. He's probably got a thing for the mom.

"You had a break in or something?"

"No, but things are changing in this area. It was quiet and safe back in the old days, but the neighborhood is changing, so you're going to need to keep a close eye on things. After today, I'm going to need you here from one to closing. You'll work the phones, schedule repairs, and

Savannah will sell the bikes. You both will close. She'll handle the paperwork, and you lock up."

Perfect.

"Got it."

Savannah comes inside and starts staring at me like she wants to eat me alive. It's a dangerous look to give to a man who's been locked up with zero conjugal visits, but that's probably the point she's trying to make clear. I can see it in her eyes. If she has any say in the matter, she wants to give me everything I've been missing for the last five years.

"Good, I need to head back home and jump in the bed before Ariana catches me. Savannah will help familiarize you with your duties. I'll come back later to close."

He blows his nose.

"I can help Savannah close today if you want."

Nate looks at Savannah then looks at me. I can tell that he thinks that I want to get my hands on his number one sales girl.

"Why?" he asks suspiciously.

"Bored," I say nonchalantly. "I'm used to keeping busy. Just want to help."

"All right then. See you later. Call me if anything comes up."

"Understood."

"Oh, and baby girl is going to bring her car in to get her backlight fixed. Don't let her leave without making sure that Sammy checks over that entire car."

"No problem."

"Make sure you teach him something on your down-time, Savannah."

"No problem, Nate," she says as she grins suggestively at me. "I'll teach the new boy here absolutely everything he needs to know."

SEVENTEEN

STONE

"What was it like in jail?"

"Predictable."

I never thought that I'd be a walking cliché, but I also never thought I'd ever end up in prison either. It's more difficult than I thought it would be to become acclimated to the real world again and it's only been a day. I've been told what to do and what time to do it for the last five years of my life. A person can get used to living like that and not know how to function otherwise. You'd think that would only happen to the old-timers, guys doing fifteen to twenty years, but it can actually happen to guys who've done even shorter bids than me.

Usually at this time of day inmates would be getting ready for another roll call and then dinner. There tended to be a scuffle or two around this time. Usually between one of the guards and a prisoner. Nothing major. At least not to a prisoner.

When you're in close quarters all day every day, with a lot of testosterone floating around, the guards tend to feel the need to put an inmate or two in check. To remind everybody who was in charge. Or sometimes it was one of the inmates wanting to prove that he couldn't be checked. So, he'd stick his chest out and instigate something. Whatever the reason, it always ended in the guard's favor, and after the show was over, the rest of us would just continue on to the mess hall like nothing ever happened.

In jail, the food is horrible and the company was even worse. The days moved slow as sludge and after a while they all seemed to just blend into one another. Just thinking about how I lived this mundane routine, day in and day out, makes me angry, mostly with myself. I got messy and I slipped up playing (as Bucky put it) Robin Hood. I should have never had all that smack in my trunk. I need to find a smarter way to hit these dealers where it hurts.

"Do girls tell you all the time that you're hot?"

Savannah's been asking me questions on and off for the last hour. Not very smart questions either. But at least we're passing time away in between the few customers that have been in the shop so far. It's boring as hell in here.

"I haven't been around women for a while."

"Oh, right. Jail and all. So, did women tell you, you were hot before you went to jail?"

"Not really."

"No? That's hard to believe," she says as she adds another coat of gloss to her lips in the mirror. "I bet they're thinking it."

"Maybe."

"Have you had any *fun* since you got here to Philly?"

"Just got here."

"I can definitely make sure you have a good time. I'm a lot of fun."

"Not right now."

"Oh." She chuckles. "I'm sorry are you gay?"

"I'm not interested in fucking you and you assume that I must be gay?"

"Hmm, you're right." She squints her eyes at me as if she's trying to solve a riddle. "You're not making my gay meter go off at all."

This girl is funny. She's probably never been turned down by a man ever in her life.

"Oh, snap!" She points her finger at me. "I know what it is. Did Nate give you the big Savannah is off limits speech?"

"He did."

"That explains it."

"Does it?" I laugh to myself.

"Of course. Five years in jail and you're passing up a taste of me? That shit didn't make any sense, but now I understand."

"You're funny."

"Listen, Stone, Nate is my boss. Not my daddy. What he doesn't know won't hurt him. I'm not looking to be somebody's wifey, I'm just living in the moment. You won't hurt my feelings if you don't want to come back for seconds. I'm totally down for a one night stand."

"No, thanks," I say again.

"You're seriously telling me that you haven't had sex with a woman in five years, and you're turning *this* down?"

She grabs a hold of her tits and holds them high.

"I don't like to mix business with pleasure."

"Your loss," she says angrily.

It's obvious that Savannah is not used to a man telling her no, but I need to make Nate feel as if he can trust me. Breaking one of the only rules that he gave me would be idiotic. Not to mention that she smells like a pack of Marlboros once you get within three feet of her.

I'm taking a closer look at one of the kick-ass, pre-owned

bikes on the floor, a Heritage Softail Classic, when I hear the bells jingle on the front door. It's a woman. She's by herself. And if I had to guess, she's probably in her early forties.

She's in pretty good shape. Nice rack. Decent face. Hell, every woman looks like a chicken dinner to me since I haven't had any real ass in a very long time. I definitely am going to have to go to a bar and get myself laid after work to take the edge off.

Savannah motions for me to come over. She seems to be relishing her role of trainer and my lord and master now that I've established that I won't be fucking her.

"We get a lot of women in here. Some are lookie-loos. Some are here to really buy. It's our job to figure out what kind of woman they are and give them what they need." I nod in understanding. "I know that I'm sales, and this is your first day, but the way that she's eyeballing you tells me that you may have a better chance of making the sale. If you succeed, you get a twenty-five percent commission. You don't want to get stuck answering phones all day in this place. You'll never make any money."

"I don't know shit about the bikes," I say in protest. Not really feeling like being thrown into the deep end so quickly.

"Doesn't matter. She doesn't know anything either. I can tell. Just try it. Oh, and put on this shirt. I found one in the back that should fit you."

The two things that you get to do in prison all day, every day, are read and work out. Since reading is like kryptonite for me, I decided to pass my time working out. I lifted weights every day, did push-ups, pull-ups and sit-ups. Needless to say, I'm ripped now. Since I'm stuck with this job, I might as well use this to my advantage.

That's why I strip from the waist up for everyone in the showroom to see, pick up my new shirt (which is a sleeveless black tee with the Harley-Davidson logo on the front and the Carter logo on the back) and walk over to the woman who just walked in and looks like she wants to sit on my face. I tuck the shirt into my waistband as I approach. Giving her a minute to gawk at my six-pack, before I put it on.

"Need help?"

She blushes.

"Umm, I'm just looking today."

"Do you know how to ride?" I ask not knowing what else to say at this point.

"Yes, I definitely do."

"Well, feel free to look around. We've got both new and pre-owned bikes available and decent financing options."

Savannah sticks her thumb up from across the room in approval.

"Thanks, um, I didn't catch your name." The corner of her mouth curves up slightly.

"Stone."

"Nice to meet you, Stone."

"Likewise."

The bells hanging on the door ring again and my eyes fly up. I want to yank those damn things off of the door. All these random bells going off every other minute are making me jumpy. Plus, I don't really feel like dealing with another lookie-loo. I'm not a big talker or bullshitter. I'm a straight shooter. And there's no way that I'm going to talk someone into spending thousands of dollars that they don't have.

But it's not a lookie-loo.

She's definitely a looker though.

It's Ariana.

Dressed in a simple black sweater and tight jeans with rips in the thighs, she looks like a goddess to me.

Not good, Stone.

I nod a quick hello to her, and start to take a walk back into the garage area to find Sammy but mostly to get away from the object of my dick's affection.

"Excuse me," she calls after me.

Dammit.

I stop dead in my tracks.

"Me?" I ask already knowing the answer.

"Umm, yes."

I turn around.

"What's up."

Ariana pauses for a moment and stares at me wide-eyed. She looks at the woman browsing around the bikes, then at Savannah, then back at me. I'm not sure if she's curious about my ink or the fact that I'm walking around shirtless in a place of business. Either way I probably look like an idiot to her. I decide that the show is over and put on my shirt.

"I brought my car in."

"I know. Your father mentioned it. I was getting Sammy for you."

"Thanks."

Ariana tells Sammy where she parked the car and gives him the key. Then we both stand around looking awkwardly at each other. I'm thinking about what I did in the shower to the fantasy of my hands all over her ass, and I have zero idea what she's thinking about, but it probably ain't good.

"Dad said you were closing tonight, so I stopped by the house and brought you some dinner." She looks over at Savannah with a look I can't quite read. "For you *and*

Savannah of course. Dad thought you two might be hungry."

"Oh, you're so sweet, Tiny. Maybe if I had known you were coming earlier I would have saved some room in here." Savannah pats her abs. "But I already had a big salad earlier and I couldn't possibly eat again."

Ariana turns what I think are disappointed eyes toward me.

"You full too?" she asks.

"I'll have a little," I say. Hating to see that look on her face. She made the effort. Someone needs to eat it.

"Okay, I'll warm it up in the back. You can eat when you're finished with your uh...customer."

Savannah giggles.

"Yeah get back over there, Casanova, and convince that woman that she needs to buy something. I'm going to pop your cherry today if it's the last thing I do."

EIGHTEEN

TINY

I never knew how much I didn't like Savannah Solomon until this very moment.

I've tolerated her backhanded comments about my weight or the fact that she dresses like some rockabilly whore for years...but this might be too much to bear. Her open and obvious flirting with Stone is making my stomach churn and starting to make me seriously consider ways I can convince my father to fire her.

Wait...somebody slap me.

This man hasn't even been in my house for more than a day, and I'm already being completely territorial. What is wrong with me? I need to pull myself together. I don't even like him.

I remove two microwavable bento boxes filled with Mediterranean styled grilled chicken, roasted veggies, and brown rice from my travel tote. Then I pull out a Ziploc bag of freshly cut pita bread and a small container of pine nut hummus made from scratch. While the food warms, I set the small card table my dad has set up for staff to eat at with a red and white checkered plastic tablecloth and some silver colored, heavy duty plastic cutlery I picked up from the dollar store. If I'm going to eat in the back of my father's bike shop, I at least would like to make the experience somewhat pleasurable.

I hear the bells on the door ring and not too shortly after, Stone appears in the back. His *customer* must have left. I quickly wonder if he was able to "pop his cherry" and get his first sale.

"You ready for me?" he asks in the grittiest voice I've ever heard.

I imagine those four words as one of the things that Stone may say right before he plunges his dick inside of a woman. But maybe these are the types of thoughts you have when you don't know any better. When you have no idea what a man says to a woman before he sleeps with them. When your only frame of reference is a Rated R movie or a steamy romance novel.

"Have a seat," I tell him. Doing my best to pretend that his mere presence doesn't affect me one iota.

Stone's eyes glaze over the meal on the table. I'm starting to think that he's always a lot hungrier than he lets on. He pulls up one of the foldable metal chairs and takes a seat. His gargantuan body is way too big for the table and chair, but he spreads his legs and tilts his body forward, so that he can get at least semi-comfortable.

"Smells good," he says.

"Hope you like it. It's just grilled chicken, veggies and hummus with pine nuts. Do you like hummus?"

"Never had it."

"Really?" I ask incredulously. "It's basically just mashed up chickpeas with tahini, garlic and olive oil."

"They don't sell hummus at the neighborhood bodegas in New York, and they definitely didn't serve it in jail."

"Oh," I say remembering that he's probably spent the last five years of his life eating crap. I may have sounded a little pretentious just now. "I apologize. Well then let me be the first to say, in the words of Savannah, it will be an honor to *pop your hummus cherry*."

I smile goofily at my bad joke. Stone doesn't crack a smile at all, but he doesn't look angry either. He just stares at me with a look that I can best describe as...confusion. He probably thinks I'm the biggest dweeb on the planet.

"Seriously though, hummus is really good and pretty healthy for you," I continue to nervously babble. "I learned how to make it a few years ago. Take a piece of pita and dip it in the hummus like a chip."

Before he grabs the pita, I stop him.

"Oh, wait a minute."

I grab some sanitizer out of my bag.

"Give me your hands."

I pour a little sanitizer in each of Stone's hands. As he holds them out for me, I notice how his palms are covered in deeply etched lines. A bold love line. A long life line. (I went through a palm reading phase when I was fourteen years old.) Each line distinct and unique from the other. I begin to wonder if those hands could talk, what wicked secrets they would hold, and in particular how they would feel touching my skin.

"I'm a little neurotic when it comes to germs," I explain. "You know I'm a nurse."

I think I see a little smirk form at the corner of his mouth.

"I'm aware."

"I mean I get to see firsthand the havoc that a little bacteria can cause."

"You don't mind letting that dog of yours lick you."

"That's different."

"Uh huh. Am I all clear now?" he asks after rubbing his hands together and holding them up for me to see. I think he's teasing me although you can never be quite sure with Stone. I'm learning that his face seems to always hold the same expression.

Clear of emotion.

Intimidating.

Beautiful.

"All clear." I look away from his face. "Let's eat."

After he takes a few bites I can tell that he's holding back, trying his best not to devour my meal. I think he may be really hungry or he really likes it. I'm not sure which it is.

"This is good," he finally says. Giving himself permission to at least enjoy it.

"I'm glad you like it. Please eat as much as you want. There's plenty since Savannah isn't eating."

He takes a long gulp of his bottled water. Watching me carefully while he slowly swallows. Holding me stock still in my seat with his stormy gray eyes.

"Why does Savannah call you Tiny?" he asks coolly.

"Umm, well that's my nickname."

"Nate doesn't call you that."

I place my fork down.

"It's not a family nickname. It's a school nickname."

"When you went to college?"

"No, high school."

I'm starting to lose my appetite from this line of questioning.

"You know Savannah from high school?"

"Yes." Unfortunately, I do.

She was always the snarky little badass in school, who had plenty of sex, yet never seemed to get a bad reputation for it. Meanwhile I was easily holding onto my virginity. In fact, I barely had a date to my prom.

"So why did Savannah, or girls like Savannah, give you that nickname?"

I take a sip of my water.

"You sure are curious about meaningless things from the past."

He stops chewing and watches me carefully.

"You don't have to tell me if you don't want."

"No–I mean it's not a big deal," I explain defensively. "It's just that...I was always a little bigger than the rest of my friends. I'm not even sure who came up with the name, but for some reason it just stuck."

"So, since they, whoever *they* were, didn't consider you a small girl they started calling you Tiny?"

I haven't given serious thought about my nickname in a long time, but now that he brings it up, I consider for a moment why I continued to allow it to follow me into adult-hood. Why did I tell my college friends that was my nick-name when they had no idea and would have never called me that if I hadn't told them? I never liked the name.

"Yes," I admit.

"Your friends could have come up with something a little more original."

"I guess."

I'm annoyed until Stone licks the seasonings from the chicken off of two of his fingers. Like an instant mood lifter, the act is almost pornographic to watch and makes me forget about everything we were just talking about.

The final lick of his thumb makes me twitch a little in my seat.

I hand him a napkin.

"I forgot to ask. Did you make the sale out there?"

"Nah, she was just looking."

"Maybe next time."

He pops a piece of pita and hummus in his mouth. Staring me down as he chews silently. I break the stare and look down at my plate.

"What time did you finally get the car?" he asks.

"It took forever. Not until about three."

"And then you went home and cooked all of this?"

"I like to cook," I say a little too defensively. This conversation reminding me way too much of Bill.

"You should like it." I pop my head back up. Is that a jab at my size?

He stares at my boobs for a second then up to my face.

"You're good at it."

Oh, he's trying to be nice.

"To be fair you'd probably like almost anything home cooked right about now."

His face hardens.

"You need to learn how to take a compliment."

"I was just—"

"Take the compliment."

"Okay," I agree quietly.

Savannah wiggles the knob to the storeroom and pops her head inside.

"Sorry to interrupt this cute little picnic you've got going on in here, but I've got a group of bikers out there and could use a hand. Stone, you coming?"

"Coming."

"Sounds like you could use a hand, Savannah," I say. "Let me just clean up and I'll help answer phones."

I can tell that she'd rather I wouldn't. She's been working here at the shop for the last three years. As far as she's concerned this is her territory and she wants me to leave, but what's she going to say to the owner's daughter? No?

"Suit yourself."

Bitch.

I take one last bite of pita and finish cleaning up our impromptu dinner. When I return to the front, I go behind the counter and work the phones like I used to every summer, before I became a full-time nurse.

Part of the reason I offered to help out tonight is because this is around the time that we get most of our service calls to the shop. People get off of work and want to bring their bikes in or check on what's happening with their repair. The other reason why I'm offering to help is not as gracious. I just don't want to leave Stone alone with Savannah. I know it makes zero sense. He's going to be working here every day and so is she. They will be alone a lot, but I guess a part of me wants to put it off as long as humanly possible.

The question is why.

I don't even like him.

NINETEEN

TINY

The air is thick with the testosterone.

Our showroom is full of bikers.

The Pennsylvania chapter of The Chosen Riders. They've been longtime customers of the shop, and it's a tradition in their club to buy a new bike for members on their ten year anniversary.

Savannah is working the room like a pro. Making sure to smile and play up her best asset (her cleavage), while Stone stands on the other side of the room watching them like a hawk. His face shows zero emotion, but his body seems as if it's stiff as a board. Maybe he doesn't like bikers or maybe he doesn't like people in general.

The same woman who was in the store when I first arrived comes over to me at the counter while keeping a close eye on Stone. I thought she had left earlier but I guess she didn't. Funny how he seems to have the same effect on women of all ages. They can't keep their eyes off of him. At least it seems as if she can't.

"Hi, can I help you?"

"The sales guy over there. Is he new here?"

"Yes, why do you ask?" Already having an idea of why she's inquiring.

"Does he do repairs?

"Actually, I'm not sure."

"I have a bike at my house that I can't get started. There's no way I'm going to be able to get it here. My old man is on a cross country haul and won't be back for a couple of weeks."

"Oh. Well I can put in a request with the service team to give you a call tomorrow and set something up."

"Why don't we ask the new guy if he'd be up for it first."

This clearly isn't just about a repair.

"Um, I'll ask him," I say reluctantly. "Stone, can you come over here a minute please?"

Stone walks over with a very serious look on his face. Like he's got a million problems. He's not going to be able to sell diddly squat with that miserable facial expression of his. I'll have to talk to him about it later. Give him some tips. Not because I want to, but if he's going to be working here, then I can't have him sabotaging sales. The income from this shop is how my father pays the bills.

"What's up."

"Um, Mrs.–"

"*Miss* Morris." She makes sure to correct me, although I'm pretty sure she already said that she has an "old man" at home.

"Sorry...*Miss* Morris is interested in a repair for her bike. Do you do them?"

"Not here."

"But you could take a look at a bike somewhere else?" she asks with hungry eyes.

"Guess so. Where is it?"

"My house. Not too far."

I have to look away for a second. This *Miss* Morris is so blatantly obvious with her agenda, that I'm embarrassed for her, even though there seems to be no shame in her game. And maybe I'm totally off base. I mean she is a good looking woman, and Stone did just get out of prison. Maybe he would totally be into a meaningless romp with her. Maybe I'm giving him too much credit in thinking that he wouldn't be interested in someone as embarrassing as this.

"I can't get the bike here, so I need someone to come and take a look at it. It's probably the engine. The thing has been sputtering for a while now."

"Write down your information, and I'll set something up with you in the next couple of days. Probably over next weekend."

Horny Miss Morris smiles as if she's hit the jackpot.

"That would be fantastic."

After she leaves the shop, I can't help but say something.

"So...am I mistaken or did you just make a date to go sleep with that woman?"

"You got all of that from that conversation?"

"Her husband is away." I move my hands casually about as I make my point. "Her engine needs fixing. It can only be done at her house. Hello?" I ball my hand in a fist and mockingly knock on the countertop. "Is anybody home? She doesn't need a bike fixed. She wants to get laid."

"She might but that's her business not mine."

"So, are you saying that you aren't going to sleep with her?"

"You think I will?"

"I don't know. That's why I'm asking."

"You think because I just got of prison that I should sleep with the first warm and willing pussy that comes my way?"

Ewww.

"I didn't say that."

"You didn't have to."

"Are you angry with the entire world or just me?"

"I'm not angry with anyone, especially you. You just fed me a bomb-ass dinner."

He even pays compliments in a unique way.

With a poker face.

Expressionless.

Hard but not heartless.

Heaven help me, but it makes me smile. Unfortunately, the small moment between us is interrupted when we both turn our heads at the sudden outburst of laughter across the room.

"Come here a minute, Stone, would you?" Savannah requests across the room in a saccharin sweet voice.

While Stone tends to Savannah's summons, one of the Chosen Riders comes over to the counter toward me. A younger member named Jake also known as Crazy Horse. He's considered a legacy in the club. Both his father and grandfather were members, which was part of the reason why he had such an infamous reputation in high school. He was a few years older than me, but I remember kids parting like the Red Sea when he would walk down the halls. Myself included.

The few times that we've run into each other as adults he's been sort of flirty, but he's never actually asked me out. I don't think he's ever been seriously interested in me. He's always dated much hotter girls than me. With me he's just playing around.

Luckily, I've always been smart enough to know the difference.

TWENTY

"**N**ice to see you again, Tiny."

I notice two missing front teeth when Jake grins at me, and it makes him look kind of trashy. He should really see about getting that fixed. From what I've heard, Chosen Riders make enough money to afford decent dental insurance.

"Hi, Jake."

He leans into the counter.

I try not to stare at the gaping hole in his smile.

"You're looking extra hot in those jeans today."

Oh, good grief. Could he be any less original?

"Thanks, Jake."

I can feel an unwavering glare from across the room. It's Stone, and he's walking over toward us with the same rigid look on his face that he's been wearing all day.

"You all right?" he asks me while looking straight down Jake's throat.

"I'm good," I say in a placating tone.

Frankly I'm a little shocked by his...I'm not sure how to explain his dominant behavior? Maybe he's taking his new job super seriously. Thinking that he's actually security in here. Another thing on my list to talk to him about. He'll scare away the clientele with that attitude. Not everyone that comes in here to buy a bike is going to be a horny, middle-aged woman looking to find her own personal Magic Mike.

"Why wouldn't Tiny be all right, new guy?" Jake questions. Offended by Stone's tone. "She's here talking to me."

Stone's posture stiffens.

Even stiffer than it was if that's even humanly possible.

"*Ariana* is on phones tonight, not sales." It doesn't get past me that he stresses the pronunciation of my first name as a direct affront to Jake's use of my nickname. "You want to buy something, you talk to Savannah. You want to shoot the shit, you call Ariana on her off time."

This is not good.

We're in a room full of Chosen Riders and Jake of all people is the wrong person to get confrontational with. Another part of his legend is that he's known for being hotheaded. Hence the nickname, Crazy Horse. I heard that one time he turned someone's car completely over on its side with his bare hands just because it had Florida plates. Evidently, he had some sort of bad bar fight in Florida that involved getting tasered by an off duty Florida State Trooper, and now he's blaming the whole entire state for it.

"The fuck you say?" Jake puffs his chest out.

Then about seven heads turn our direction. All featuring varying degrees of scowls across them. All wearing Chosen Rider cuts.

"Jake, he didn't mean—"

Stone places his hand on my forearm. Resting it there for a moment. Essentially shushing me.

"I think you heard every word I said," he says to Jake.

"Keep it the fuck moving. This is a place of business. Not a bar."

It's so quiet in the shop you can hear a pin drop.

"Is this disrespectful cocksucker your old man, Tiny?" Jake asks. Spittle practically flying out of his mouth, as he asks his question with a mouth full of missing teeth and fury.

I need to be really careful here. However I decide to answer Jake and the other seven Chosen Riders who are listening to this exchange is going to determine whether or not there's about to be a bloodbath in my father's shop.

If I tell the truth and tell Jake that Stone is nothing to me, Jake is probably going to hurt Stone and I cannot have that. My father would have a hissy fit and like it or not, Stone is a guest in my home. So maybe if I lie and say yes, then the riders will walk away out of respect for me or at least for my father. He's been a longtime friend of the club.

"Yes, he—"

"It doesn't fucking matter who I am," Stone replies before I can lie. I watch as Stone's eyes grow an icier gray color. The angrier he grows the more lethal looking he gets. Like a lone wolf. A lone sexy wolf.

Before I can do or say anything to diffuse the situation, Savannah suddenly bolts over and physically plants herself and those double D's of hers in between Stone and Jake. Something I should have done ten seconds ago myself. This heifer is always beating me to the punch.

"Come on, boys. This is supposed to be a ten year celebration for Max. Let's focus our energies on picking him out the baddest badass bike in the shop. I've got a bottle of tequila in the back once the paperwork is signed."

Savannah splays her palm on Jakes chest. "Because of the break ins around here lately, Stone's been helping out with security. He's just taking his new job a little too seriously. He doesn't realize that we're the safest that we'll ever be with you boys in here."

Savannah laughs nervously. Making sure to stick her boobs out when she does. I have to give it to her, she knows how to talk to men. Especially these types of men. I hear a couple of "hell yeah you are" and "fucking right" from several of the bikers after Savannah's speech which seems to have calmed the waters.

Jake stares for another long moment at Stone, taps his hand on the counter one time and finally turns to me. "Are you working here tomorrow, Tiny, or at the hospital?"

I've got the feeling that what just transpired between Jake and Stone has just ignited an interest in me that was barely fleeting ten seconds ago. Last thing I need is a damn toothless biker popping up at my job and asking around for me.

"I have to check my schedule. The shifts change around so much."

I just made that up. I actually know my schedule for the next thirty days.

"Your next day off it's me and you." Then he eyeballs Stone. "And it would probably be best if you leave your new bodyguard here at home. Watch your back, fucker."

Stone responds with a chilling smirk that makes my insides rattle.

"Likewise."

STONE

MARCH

I'm not one of those people that can run for the sake of running. I have to have a purpose. That's why three times a week, I make sure to run with a destination in mind. Today I'm running to a juice bar that's about a mile's run from the house. The angry dude who works the juicer is fixing me a carrot and spinach juice bomb. Some overpriced shit that's supposed to help me keep my energy levels up.

I'm patiently waiting for my drink and playing on my phone when someone taps me on my shoulder. I'm pissed when I realize who it is. Not just because I don't want to talk to this motherfucker, but because I should have seen this pirate in a three piece suit coming a mile away.

"What's up, Stone."

"What are you doing here?"

"Checking in on my client. Do you have my money yet?"

"Not yet."

"Are you close to getting my money?"

"What's the rush?"

"Rush? You've owed me my money for five fucking years. I think I've been pretty patient about things if you ask me."

The tone of Bucky's voice garners us a bit of unwanted attention. Usually I wouldn't care about shit like that, but I've found myself giving a shit about what people think more than I think I ever have. Particularly what one person thinks.

"I've been working for Nate for over a month now–"

"Correction–living and working."

So, he does have eyes on me.

"Right–living and working and I don't see any evidence of any money. His house is modest. His car is modest. No other properties. In fact, so far, it looks to me as if his bike shop is barely breaking even year to year."

Bucky turns his lips up to one side.

"Now who would keep a shop open that's just breaking even for thirty damn years. That doesn't make any common sense, and if there's one thing I know about Nate Carter it's that he isn't dumb."

"He may not be stupid, but he definitely is sentimental. I definitely think he might be holding onto the shop, because it means something to his family. It's his legacy."

"All that family shit doesn't matter. He can keep that bike shop for the next millennium. That doesn't negate the fact that I want my money. So, find it or move to plan B. You've got four months left."

I nod my head in understanding, as I look anxiously through the glass pane of the store. I don't want to let on to Bucky, but there's a very specific reason why I've come to the juice bar today. Ariana is going to be here in about ten minutes.

Even though Nate and Ariana live in a nicely sized

house, you can hear a lot through those walls, especially when she gets on the phone. She probably doesn't realize how much I can hear downstairs, because she's never lived with anyone but her father, and he never talks on the phone.

She probably also doesn't realize that when she's talking to a man, except for me, that she uses a certain tone of voice. A gentler voice. Like she's trying to pretend that she's some sort of delicate flower. I hate it. She doesn't use that voice with me. With me it's either all business or she says practically nothing at all.

It's in this muted little voice, I overheard her agreeing to meet the man here today. I don't know who it is, but until I see otherwise, I can only assume it was the douchebag biker whose lungs I almost kicked into next week that time at the shop. If it is him there's going to be some shit that goes down in this juice bar today, and I can't have Bucky seeing any of that.

"Are we done?"

He squints his one good eye at me suspiciously, grabs his order from angry guy, and motions to leave.

"Done for now."

I wait until Bucky is out of view and then I take a seat in the farthest corner of the store that I can. The place is almost packed with people, so I'm hoping that once my hoodie is up she won't notice that I'm here.

"Is anyone sitting here?" A woman with short blond hair and a yoga outfit on asks.

"No, you want the chair?"

"I thought I'd sit with you. You look like you could use the company."

Sometimes I feel like I've been in jail for fifty not five years. I didn't realize that women were so forward these days. I mean I definitely was never hurting for female attention, but lately they seem to be coming at me left and right.

"You can sit. Not interested in talking though."

You'd think that would be enough to send her on her way, but the woman sits down anyway with her drink and some sort of disgusting looking brown muffin and starts rambling.

"I'm Patricia."

I give her a head nod and then look back at my phone. I've been spending the last few weeks playing around with apps and on social media sites. Getting familiar with online jargon and laughing at fight videos. These kids are stupid posting videos of themselves fighting and robbing people, and they're not even good at it.

"What kind of drink is that you have?"

I sigh and look back up from my phone. Is she really going to talk me to death?

"Carrot and spinach bomb."

"Oh, that one's healthy. I've got a fruity one. A little more natural sugar in it than yours. I was in the mood for mangos today."

Out of the corner of my eye I see her.

And my body starts to vibrate simply because she is in the building.

She's meeting the guy here after having already worked an overnight shift and is dressed in a pair of purple scrubs, work clogs, and all of her tightly coiled curls are pushed back with some sort of thin gold headband then swept up in a ponytail. When she peels off her parka and places it on the back of her chair, I can't help but salivate at the curves trying to burst their way through her scrubs.

She looks like a snack.

I throw the hood of my Target brand navy blue hoodie

up and take another sip of my juice. My table mate continues to ramble on about something. The price of gas or the new construction on the corner of Chestnut Street. I'm not really sure, and it doesn't even fucking matter, because I can't keep my eyes off of Ariana.

She keeps looking out the front window for what I suppose is dickhead biker, but am proven wrong when a man in different colored scrubs and a white jacket sits down at the table with her. Obviously, a doctor. For a split second, I assumed that this was a business meeting, but that crooked grin spread across his face when he sits down directly opposite her tells me everything that I need to know. Predators know they're own kind.

This is not business.

This is monkey business.

I can feel the insides of my body vibrating as I watch him. The way I imagine Bottle feels when she's stalking the neighbor's cat through the living room window. The prey drive in her is undeniable. She wants to get to that cat. She wants to chase him. Catch him. Shake him. Kill him. But she can't. She's stuck in the house with us. A prison of sorts. Stopping her from doing what her ancestral code is compelling her to do.

Take out the enemy.

Am I just like Bottle? Is this all about some primitive part of me that is driving my decision making? I'm not really sure. Some of it probably has to do with the fact that after living with Ariana for weeks, I still don't know that much about her and that shit bothers me. She routinely avoids me. Only talking to me when it's necessary. Do I need anything from the store? Am I eating dinner? Do I have any clothes that need to be washed?

At first, I thought this purposeful distance she was

putting between us was a blessing. I don't need to form any attachments to her. I don't need to get to know her. Just on the off chance that I'd have to move to plan B, I don't want some sort of personal fondness for her to become a barricade to the main objective.

Saving my ass.

TWENTY-TWO

TINY

"Why did you want to meet in person, Bill?"

"I talked to my sister and she has some good assignments available, but there's one in Rhode Island that I think would be the perfect match. You're going to like this assignment a lot. It's in a small town. You'd have a permanent bed in the local bed and breakfast that the hospital would pay for. And this is no half-assed mom and pop B and B. This place has been in *Town & Country Magazine*."

"How nice for them, but why would you think I'd like it there?"

"This B and B is known for their cuisine."

I raise my eyebrows.

"You're interested now, aren't you?" He grins. "The daughter of one of the owners ended up marrying a world-renowned chef from Portugal, and he cooks there on the weekends. There's a waiting list to eat there on weekends. Just for this guy. But you'd get to eat it all the time, because you'd be living there. Meals are part of the boarding arrangement. Sweet, right?"

"I have to admit, Bill. I'm impressed. This actually does sound like it may be a good fit for me. Room and board. Not too far from home but far enough. Thank you. But why couldn't I just talk to your sister about this position? She never responded to my email or my call."

Bill squirms a little in his chair.

Then he places a hand on top of mine.

"Because I told her not to."

Huh?

"And why would you do that, Bill?"

"I'm going to be honest with you, Tiny. I'm part owner in the B and B. A small investment I made years ago that ended up being a great one. If you took the assignment there, I could come see you on the weekends when I'm not working in Philly. I could show you Rhode Island. I've been vacationing there all my life. In fact, we could explore the entire New England Coast if you want."

"When did you buy into a B and B?"

"It's part of my retirement plan. That's where I want to end up retiring. I love it there."

"Oh, I see."

"Doesn't it sound amazing?"

Yeah, for a married couple.

"We broke up, Bill."

"I know, but that wasn't something I wanted. That was all you. I've been thinking about it a lot lately and I think I know why you ended things."

Because there was nothing to end.

Because you're a selfish jerk.

Because you're a narcissistic workaholic.

"I played a part in that." That you did. "And the weirdness for us at the hospital didn't make matters any better. But the great thing about Rhode Island is that nobody really knows us there. We can be who we want to be. I'll be working here. You'll be working there. It's perfect."

It's interesting to me how he thinks that he has come up with such an amazing plan for us to be together, and it does nothing but make feel even worse than I did before. He wants to date me in a place where no one knows us? Oh yeah, that makes me feel real wanted.

"Why do you want to get back together with me?"

"Because we'd make a great power couple. If things work out, and if you decided to relocate to Rhode Island, in a couple of years I could open a small private practice and you could be my supervising nurse."

I try sliding my hand from under his. This whole conversation is making me ill. I was an idiot for reaching out to him in the first place. This is no longer about helping me find a traveling placement. Some kind of way this has been twisted around and made about him. Bill always finds a way to make any situation about Bill.

"No, Bill."

"No?"

"I have zero interest in continuing a romantic relationship with you."

"What? Why?"

"I'm just not interested."

"I need more than that, Tiny. Use your words."

This condescending bastard.

"What the hell did you just say to me?"

"You're an educated woman. I'm asking for you to explain to me why you're still saying no, and I'm giving you everything you want. I'm offering you the world and it's still not enough."

At this point he's holding on to my arm and keeping it

on the table. I try again to yank my arm from out of his grip but he grabs my wrist.

"Don't run from me, Tiny."

"Bill, let go."

"I don't want to let you go. Can't you see that? I'm fighting for us. Isn't that what you've always wanted?"

Before I can tell him to take his warped version of fighting for me and shoving it up his butthole, I can feel a huge shadow hovering behind me. And that smell. It's familiar. A spicy blend of bergamot, musk and vanilla.

"Get your hands off of her."

Stone.

I'd know that angry, raspy voice anywhere.

And now my anxiety level has ratcheted from zero to one hundred in ten seconds flat.

"Excuse me?" Bill responds.

"I said take your hands off of Ariana, or I'll do it for you."

Bill looks visibly shook as he lifts his hands off of my wrist.

"Settle down," I say to Stone. "We were just talking. There's no problem here."

I try scooting my chair back, so that I can stand up and talk to Stone on the side, but he walks up closer to me. Caging me in against the table. I can't move.

"Stone, I can't get up."

"Stay where you are then."

"Let me up."

"No."

"I'm calling the police," Bill says as he pulls out his phone.

"No!" I plead. "Everything's fine. Put your phone down."

"Am I missing something, Tiny? I can't touch your arm but this guy can hold you hostage. Who is this jackass?"

"Don't call her that."

"I called *you* the jackass. Not her."

"You called her Tiny."

"That's her name, genius," Bill says sarcastically.

"Her name is Ariana Carter. You can call her Miss Carter, or you can never call her anything again after I shove those oversized white veneers of yours down your chickenshit throat."

TWENTY-THREE

TINY

"Stone!"

Why is he so off of the rails today?

"Please go back to wherever you came from and mind your business. You're embarrassing me."

"No."

"I'm not asking, son of Jack."

"When he goes, then I'll go."

"This is ridiculous, *Tiny*. If you don't explain to me who this is in ten seconds, I'm calling the cops."

"I live with her," Stone says with a smirk. "Can't you tell?" He's purposely trying to give Bill the wrong idea about us.

I shove back with all my might. I just want to turn around and throttle him, but he doesn't budge. In fact, he bends over and brushes his lips against the side of my face. Dangerously brushing them close to the valley between my shoulder and my neck.

"You're not going anywhere," he growls with authority in my ear.

Goose bumps start to rise on the back of my neck, and

the vibration of his threat goes straight to my core. My throat feels too parched to allow me to speak.

"I'm sorry, Bill, but do you mind if we continue this conversation later."

Bill looks at me, then Stone, then me again.

"Are you serious? I'm talking about a future with you, and you're just going to let this overdeveloped thug interrupt us."

"A future, huh? I thought you didn't have a man," Stone says to me.

I try whipping my head around, but it's hard with two hundred and fifty pounds of muscle holding my body in one place.

"I never said that."

"I distinctly remember you saying at breakfast that you weren't seeing the biker. That you weren't seeing anyone."

"Breakfast? And what biker?!"

"She never told you about the biker?"

"Stone Barringer, you are acting completely out of pocket right now. I'm going to kill you when I finally get out of this chair."

"Ariana evidently has men interested in her by the dozens. Also, I made a promise to her father that I'd look out for her best interest, and you don't seem to be it. It would probably be best for you to let this go. She's not the one for you."

Stone leans back over.

"Don't ever tell anyone my last name again," he whispers.

I slam my hand on the table, because I don't have enough room to turn around and slap him with it.

"Go. Away. Convict."

I know that was kind of a low blow, but at this point the

entire juice bar is looking at us. People come here for the laid back vibe and nutritious smoothies, and we're giving them a show worthy of a reality show award. If those even exist. I've had enough.

Bill gains his composure and takes a look at all the glances from around the room. He doesn't like negative attention. It doesn't mesh well with his sensibilities. He stands up and begins to smooth the sides of his white lab coat. Something he does when he's trying to calm himself.

"We'll talk about this later, Tiny."

"Bye." Stone facetiously waves.

I don't think I've ever seen his face or heard his voice so animated in the short time that I've known him. He actually is getting some sort of sick enjoyment out of this.

Of course, he is, you idiot, he's a criminal.

As soon as Bill exits the bar, Stone slides into the seat opposite me, with some sort of look on his face that I've never seen before. Just like I don't know what he's thinking when he's wearing one of his frozen, expressionless faces, I damn sure don't know what he's thinking now that there's some movement. It's quite peculiar.

"You can do better than him," he states as if he's actually giving me some gems and jewels on how to pick men.

"Are you on drugs?"

"Wouldn't you be able to tell if I was?"

"That was a rhetorical question."

"I'm not used to rhetorical questions. Don't use them with me. I'm used to actual questions that people want actual answers to."

"It's apparent that you're used to prison life. In the real world, there is more than black and white. There are many shades of gray, and that's where sarcasm lives. If you want to have a conversation with me, you're going to have to get used to it. I try not to pass judgment on you because you've done time, but you were a terrible bully today. We're not in the freakin' penitentiary mess hall. Don't act like that again."

"I heard you say the word no, and then I saw his hand still on you. You were pulling away. He wouldn't let go. If there was anyone being a bully in here this morning it was him."

"Last time I checked I didn't have a secret service detail."

"You should. You've got men coming after you left and right. I can't keep up with them all."

"Then don't keep up! Mind your business."

"How was your shift today?"

"Really? You're making small talk now."

"You seem tired."

I counter like I'm in a debate with a five-year-old.

"Shut up. You seem tired."

And at that response Stone laughs.

I mean an actual cackle comes out of his gargantuan body.

A big belly laugh.

It puts a smile on almost everyone in the bar as they watch him.

"Shut up," I say through some stilted laughter of my own. "Shut up."

He quiets down, but there's still a huge grin on his face.

"I can't help it. You make me laugh."

His face grows serious again.

"You make me feel."

Then Stone does something completely unexpected.

He leans his elbows on the table and extends his right arm to cradle the side of my face. He uses his thumb to lightly rub both of my lips until he gently pries them apart.

"You make me want."

The green smoothie in my stomach starts doing somersaults.

The hand that's cupping the side of my head pulls me forward as he does the same. Meeting together in the center of our small table. I gasp. Totally unprepared for what is happening between us right now.

He kisses me gently. Almost reverently. And when an indescribable moan comes from somewhere inside of me, the kiss becomes more aggressive. Passionate. Hungry.

I close my eyes as I free fall more deeply into the kiss, but he grips my hair in his fist. "Look at me, Ariana." Pulling my head back and forcing me to look at him.

"Don't worry. When I fuck you, you're going to forget all about whoever that was who just left here."

I laugh.

"Oh, is that funny?"

"You're not going to ever have the privilege of fucking me, son of Jack."

"Oh, it's obvious. Trust me. I'm going to be the master of the next orgasm you have. You can decide how that's going to happen. It can happen while I'm inside of you or while you're alone thinking about me in the shower."

"Then I guess I pick the shower."

"That's the wrong decision. You seem to be making a lot of those these days. It will feel so much better with me inside of you."

"I highly doubt that."

"Are you actually scared of me?"

"Yes."

"I would never hurt you."

"No, you definitely would."

"Ariana—"

"It seems as if you're missing a critical piece of information."

"What? What am I missing?"

"I don't think you'd hurt my heart–I think you'd hurt my body." I lower my voice to barely a discernible decibel level. "Stone, I'm a virgin."

<<<<>>>>

TWENTY-FOUR

STONE

APRIL

There is no fucking money.

I've spent the last few weeks frustrating the fuck out of myself. Meticulously sifting through Nate Carter's life with a fine tooth comb. Working my ass off at the shop. Getting to know every technician there and subtly questioning them about Nate. Searching the house for bank or insurance records when no one is home. Scouring through Nate's Internet search history. Sucking up to Savannah. And I got nothing.

He has three bank accounts. One business checking, one personal checking, and one savings. Combined they clear about a hundred and fifty-five thousand dollars. There's no investment accounts. No stocks. No expensive art or gun collection. No stamps or coins. Nothing. Nate lives a very normal middle class life.

But something doesn't add up.

Ariana did not go to college on scholarship nor did she take out any loans. Nate paid for her education completely out of pocket. I saw the statements. An education at an Ivy League school runs at a minimum of sixty thousand dollars a year. That's not including dorm fees and everything else. Any way you slice it, that's a lot of money to cough up every year over a four year span from a business that according to his taxes hasn't made much of a profit in the last seven years.

A part of me feels terribly conflicted about this. On one hand, I hate drug dealers. Especially heroin dealers. Bucky was right about that. I've never been able to verify it, but I heard the same story from three different social workers who decided to break all types of privacy laws.

My mother was a heroin addict. An addict of the worst kind who was caught trying to sell me to a sex porn peddler. Any mother who would sell their child to someone like that has to be out of her mind. Out of her mind because some-body made her that way. Probably a lot of somebody's. But for me it starts and ends with the drug dealer who sold her her very first hit. So yeah, it's personal for me. Personal as fuck.

So, if that's who Nate is, if that's how he's made his money over the years, then he should pay. He shouldn't reap the benefits of destroying people's lives. People's souls. He should lose every single cent of that blood money.

On the other hand, I was hoping that I didn't find any money because truth be told, I like Nate. I think he's a good man, a fair boss, and a great father. It's hard for me to believe that someone like him was a drug runner. Even in his youth. Part of me wants to believe that Bucky is fucking with me. That this is all a game to him and that he's just doing this to get me to unknowingly run off one of the last few people in my life that actually gives two fucks about me.

But of course, if that's true, if Nate doesn't have any drug money, then that means I'm up shit's creek. I still owe a man seven million dollars, and I have no way to get it, which means that I would be forced to move forward with plan B. A plan which at this point I know that I could never follow through with, because if I attempt to make Ariana fall in love with me, there's no way that I'm going to be able to break her. In fact, it's the total other way around. She would be the one with the power to break me.

That's why ever since that day at the juice bar, I have had to slide my mask back on. Keeping things cordial, platonic, and respectful. She hates it. She hates me. She thinks I'm rejecting her. And she probably thinks I am because she told me she's a virgin. A twenty-five-year-old goddamn virgin.

Okay, I admit that was a mind blower. I mean she's had to have had horny little fuckers trying to tap that since she hit puberty. And I wouldn't be telling the truth if I didn't admit that part of me is petrified of what would happen if I did sleep with her.

If I was her first lover. The first inside? The first man to teach her how to ride on top? The first lover to put her on all fours and hit walls and muscles she never knew were there? The first guy to lift her juicy ass up and fuck her good and proper against a shower wall? If I think it's difficult to keep away from her now, getting inside of that shiny new pussy of hers would turn something primal on in me for sure.

So, you forget about *breaking her* per Bucky's orders. I wouldn't be able to let her go. And that will not only get me killed, but it would put her in serious danger too. And the thought of anything happening to someone as innocent as Ariana is just too much to bear.

I might as well lay down and die.

"What are you doing home?" she asks.

I can hear the venom in her voice when she speaks to me.

"Your father is at the shop, and so is your little friend Jake. It was decided amongst the staff that I should leave early for the day."

She rolls her eyes.

"Jake is harmless. You should let that rest."

"And you should stay away from him."

"My father actually likes Jake. He'd probably give me his blessing if I gave him first crack at it."

I crack my knuckles. A bad habit I picked up in jail. I know she's fucking with me, but she's pushing me to my limits when she talks like that.

"What are you cooking?" I ask changing the subject.

"I'm baking a red velvet cake with cream cheese frosting."

"What's wrong?" I ask as I walk over to dip my finger into the cake batter.

She slaps my hand back.

"Wash your hands, convict."

I chuckle and move to the sink to start washing my hands.

"What makes you think that there's anything wrong? You sound like Nathaniel Carter right now."

"You cook for fun. You bake to forget something."

I shut her up with that. She thinks I don't know her, that I don't pay attention, but even when she gives me the silent treatment, I learn more about Ariana each and every day.

"I applied for a job that I didn't get."

Finally, a real conversation.

"What kind of job? I thought you loved your job."

"I'm applying for a traveling nurse position."

"A traveling nurse?"

"It's simply a placement of a nurse into an area with a nurse shortage. We get paid a great hourly wage and usually your housing is subsidized."

"So, you're leaving?"

"That was the plan, but you ruined the first opportunity I had when you ran Bill out of the juice bar. His sister owned the agency that was going to get me a prime placement. Now neither he or her will return my calls. He walks right by me in the hospital."

"Aww, that's too bad."

"You're such a jerk. Bill is actually a big deal in this town. I think he may have even put the word out with some of the other agencies not to hire me. There's no way that I shouldn't have gotten that job today."

"Maybe you don't interview well."

"Oh my God! Shut up and get out of my kitchen."

"I'm just saying you're being a little presumptuous. You think you're the only qualified nurse in the city of Philadelphia?"

"You get a kick out of seeing me suffer or something?"

"You're suffering working at one of the premier hospitals in the city? Making a super high five figure salary. Living rent free in a renovated house."

"I may not have done time like you," she says as she vigorously mixes the batter. "But there are times that I feel like I am."

Her eyes get a little glassy.

"What do you mean, Ariana?"

I place my hand on hers and stop her from churning the damn batter into butter.

"I'm suffocating in this house."

"Because of me?"

"No, my house is like a living memorial to my mother.

And yes, while it's heart wrenching, and sweet, and romantic, it's painful as shit for me. He talks about her a hundred times a day. He compares everything I do to her. My cooking, the way I clean, how I talk, a joke I may tell, an outfit I may wear, the way I may laugh. It's exhausting. So, I need to get away. I need to breathe."

"Why don't you tell him."

"And break his heart? I couldn't. He's done so much for me. He lives to make me happy. I know that. So how would I sound telling him to stop grieving for my mother. How much of an asshole would I sound like?"

"Don't go, Ariana. Just talk to him."

One lone tear rolls down her face.

I catch it with my thumb and wipe it away.

"You'll get tears in the batter."

"Be quiet, son of jack. Just...be quiet."

TWENTY-FIVE

STONE

I'm in the storeroom in the back of the shop when I hear the front door bells jingle. My dick grows instantly hard. A cruel joke being played on me by a part of my human anatomy that thinks it's party time every time it learns that it will see Ariana, because we don't see her often.

That's my fault.

When she lets her guard down, and reveals a little part of herself to me, I pull back. First it was her virginity and then it was her true feelings about living in the shadow of her mother's ghost. Both times I ran for the hills. Not because I'm an asshole, but because the more she shares with me, the more I want to take care of her. And I'm in no position to take care of her. In fact, I'm probably her biggest problem, because Bucky is definitely watching.

I can feel it.

Most of the time the two of us are like two ships passing in the night. We work similar shifts and when she comes home, she cooks, she may utter a few sentences to me and then she crashes. Tonight though, my dick is all excited because she's coming in to close up the shop for Nate who is out of town for three days at a Harley convention.

Savannah has been in a mood all day about it. Probably because she feels slighted. She thinks that Nate should trust her enough to do it herself, and she's right, but Nate has some serious control issues when it comes to his business and that's just one more thing that doesn't sit right with me.

He runs his business like a drug dealer would run their business.

Only trusting themselves and close family. Never an outsider.

I haven't heard more than ten sentences come out of Ariana's beautiful mouth in so long, that I decide to eavesdrop for a little while before I come out and ruin it all. I'm sure she'll immediately clam up as soon as she sees me.

"Hey, Savannah."

"Hey."

"How was business today?"

Ariana sounds exhausted.

"Slow."

"Did we sell anything?"

"No, *we* didn't sell anything, but *I* booked two rentals. Anything else, boss?"

It irks me that Savannah is talking to Ariana like that, but I know that my girl can handle herself. So I fall back.

"Is there something you want to say to me, Savannah, because I just worked a long shift and I'm really not in the mood for your attitude."

"Oh, is that right? Someone is feeling a little high and mighty lately isn't she."

"What is your freakin' problem?"

"Well since you asked. I've been working here for three years making most of the sales in this dead-ass place, and your father doesn't trust me enough to close out the books? He always has to do it or have you do it. What the hell, Tiny? Does he think I'm going to steal someone's credit card numbers, or that I don't know how to count end of the night sales figures? Maybe I didn't go to Penn like you, but I do have a high school degree."

"I don't know what he's thinking, Savannah. You'd have to talk to him about that. You think I feel like coming here after I've worked a twelve-hour shift, then going back home to that mausoleum, and then getting back up the next day and doing the shit all over again?!"

"AHHHH!!!"

I jump when I hear the blood curdling screams of both women.

Are they fighting?

I haul ass out of the room, but don't find two women rolling around on the floor like I assumed I would. What I find are three men with black ski masks. One has a gun pointed on Savannah. The other has one pointed on Ariana. And the third has one aimed right at my head. I walked right into it. And now we're fucked, because all of the technicians have gone for the day. It's just me and the girls.

"On the floor, motherfucker," he orders.

I put my hands up and get slowly down on my knees flicking my eyes back and forth between the gun aimed at my head and the one pointed at Ariana.

Tears are streaming down her face.

It wrecks me.

I want to run to her, hold her, and assure her that I won't let them touch a hair on her head, but if I do that, I'd be revealing that I give a shit specifically about her, and then they'd probably use it against me. So I stand down.

"You're going about this all wrong," I say to the one holding the 45 on me. He's definitely the one in charge.

"Where's the safe, asshole."

"This is a Harley dealership. Not a fucking 7-Eleven," I say coldly. "We don't have a safe. All our transactions are through a credit card processor."

"Shut the fuck up and take me to the safe."

This doesn't make sense.

Either this guy is really stupid or he actually knows that there's a safe in here.

"There's no safe," I reiterate.

He presses the barrel of the gun into my temple, but I continue to stare him down. If he's going to kill me then this is where it's going to happen. I will gladly lay my life down for Ariana. I've laid down my life for much less.

"Wait!" Ariana cries out. "I know where it is."

What the fuck is she talking about.

"Take me to it."

The guy on Ariana and the asshole on me switch places. Ariana stands up and looks at me with mascara running down her face. Fear in her eyes. But not just fear for herself. Fear for me as well. It's a look that I'll never forget. The look of someone who actually gives a damn about my well-being.

She doesn't guide the guy to the storeroom like I assumed she would, but walks right behind the front counter and lifts up the industrial all-weather mat that's on the floor back there. She points to a trap door which is hidden underneath it. The only place I didn't think to look when I was looking for whatever I could on Nate.

"What you want is down there."

STONE

"I can't open it."

Ariana is exhausted. What little energy she had left after working a long shift at the hospital is being drained from her because of this clusterfuck.

"Why not?"

"I don't have the key."

"Well where's the fucking key?"

He points the gun closer to her face.

I could smash his head like a pumpkin into the concrete countertop, but that still leaves the two other dickheads with guns in their hands. I can't risk it.

"My father is the only one with a key. I just know that the safe is down there."

"The key's probably at her house, man." One of the other men says. I notice that he has a tattoo of a wolf on his hand. "But that shit is like thirty minutes away."

They know a lot. Too much. They know about the safe. They know that Ariana lives with Nate. They even know where they live. This shit isn't good. I can't allow them to leave this place breathing.

"It's not there," she says fearfully. "My father always carries it on him, and he's out of town."

"I don't believe her."

"Me either."

The one in charge is thinking it over. He didn't anticipate this kink in the plan, but that's the thing about armed robbery. You always have to consider the possibilities and plan for contingencies, and even then, you're taking a huge risk.

"Everybody up," the leader orders.

We all stand and he has Savannah and I walk over to the trap door, making sure to put me in front.

"Open the door," he tells me.

I lift the trap door and find exactly what Ariana said. Steps to a dark cellar. There's a light switch at the top of the stairs and it works. Nate must come down here occasionally. At least to change the bulb. Each of us descends down the stairs, and I'm shocked at what we find when we reach the bottom.

A safe that looks like it's the size of a fucking bank vault built into the stone wall of the basement.

Fuck me.

This is where he's keeping the money.

"Sit down."

They order all three of us to sit on the floor of the cellar while they take a look at the safe. It doesn't require a key. It's a huge combination lock. Just like you would see on an old school bank vault. Ariana has just been caught in a lie. Making our amateur thieves even angrier than they already were.

"I thought you said this was a key lock!"

"I thought it was," she cries. "My father told me it was."

"You expect us to believe that shit. You've never seen this safe in your life? You knew where the trap door was."

"I've never been down here though. He told me about the safe. Told me where it was in case something ever happened to him. But that's it."

"How about you?" they ask Savannah.

"I didn't even know this cellar existed, and I've worked here for years. They don't tell me shit."

I look around and notice there are several things down here besides a safe. There are a couple of old wooden closet doors, an out of service dehumidifier, a rusted oil fuel tank, and some old copper piping left on the ground.

I think I could take at least two of them out with one of the pipes but not all three of them. One of them would definitely have time to shoot me in the head or worse one of the girls. I need to separate these bozos, but I have to think of a smart way how and soon. There's no way they're going to get in that safe, and then they're going to be left with the task of figuring out what to do with us.

And then serendipity strikes.

We all hear them the moment they chime. Those idiots forgot to lock the door, and now someone has entered the shop. We hear the heavy footsteps of at least two or three booted men. Right above our heads.

"Savannah! Where you at?!"

The voice sounds familiar and for once I'm glad to hear it. It's Jake from the Chosen Riders and it sounds like two of his friends.

"Fuck!" one of the masked men says.

"Stay quiet," the leader warns us, "or you're all dead."

Both girls look at me with desperation in their eyes. I know it's now or never. I reach for one of the copper pipes and swing around hitting the guy on me at the knees. He jerks back and his gun goes off as he falls to the floor.

"Run!" I yell to the girls as I wrestle with the leader for his gun. He gets a good shot in and knocks me in the back of the head with the butt of his gun before I get it from him.

Finally, I hear what I've been hoping for.

Thunderous footsteps finding the door behind the counter and running down the steps with guns drawn. First Jake and then Max. Then two minutes later there are five more bikers behind them.

"Put your guns down, assholes, or you die right where you stand."

My guy stops moving and drops his gun to the ground.

I touch the back of my head and discover blood as a result of the blow to my head; just because I'm completely furious that he got a lucky hit, I punch him dead in his face and knock him the fuck out.

I run over to Ariana who at this point looks shell-shocked. Jake is trying to ask her questions she can't answer, while some of the other Chosen Riders tie the assailant's arms back with plastic ties and lead them up the stairs.

"Where are they taking them?" I ask Jake.

"Away."

"They know where she lives," I say to him. Knowing he'll understand what that means.

"Not anymore," he promises.

Then I scoop Ariana up in my arms and get her the fuck out of there. I don't even give a shit about the safe or the store. I need to get my girl back home where she belongs.

TWENTY-SEVEN

TINY

MAY

"You tired?"

"A little. I pulled a long shift."

It's been a few weeks since the robbery attempt at the shop and while I'm not looking over my shoulder every ten seconds like I was before, I still feel discombobulated and confused. The three of us almost lost our lives because of something they thought was in my father's safe, and he's so shook by it, that he refuses to discuss it. At least not with me. More than ever before, I want to leave this house.

"What do you usually do to relax?"

"You already know what I do. Cook or bake. Watch TV. Read. Sometimes I go clubbing with my friends, but that's kind of quieted down since Elizabeth got pregnant."

"Who's Elizabeth?"

"She's one of my closest friends from college."

"I never hear you talk about her."

"I've been out of touch with my friends for a while. I work a lot. I like to keep busy."

"You're not running from me, are you?"

I'm a nurse. I know that something's wrong with me. I've been through something traumatic, and I'm having some difficulty processing it. Not only am I shaken by the fact that I almost died in a cold, damp cellar, but when I relive the whole thing, I burst out in tears when I think about how I almost watched Stone get shot in the head. The only reason why I didn't totally lose it down there was because of the look he had on his face when that gun was being pressed into his temple.

He was calm.

Eerily calm.

And in turn it gave me a sliver of hope that we could possibly make it out of there. Even if The Chosen Riders hadn't come, I know that Stone was prepared to fight each and every one of those criminals to the death if it came to that.

"Everything isn't always about you, Stone."

"I'm just saying. I can count on my hands the number of times you've been here in the last few weeks. You seeing somebody I don't know about?"

I could have sworn that he just asked that with a jealous edge to his voice, but Stone always has an edge to his voice. I chalk that up to me being pathetic and hearing what I want to hear.

"I didn't realize you were counting."

"I think you meant to say that you didn't realize I could count."

"I never said you were a moron."

"That was supposed to be a joke."

"Oh, well you're not good at them. Keep practicing."

I put down my things and begin to make myself a cup of coconut and mango herbal tea. It's one of my favorites.

"You want some?" I ask since he seems to be watching me so intently. He's really picking up a lot of bad habits from my father.

"No, I'm just watching."

"Always watching," I mutter under her breath.

"Come sit with me after you fix your tea," he orders in a deeper voice than normal.

I kick off my shoes and enter his room with my tea cup. Slowly mixing my blossom honey in with a small spoon as I walk. It's already completely dissolved, but I'm nervous. So I stir.

The room looks almost exactly like it did when he moved in. Clean. Neat. Sparse. The sheets on his bed are smoothed and pulled tight with military precision, two pairs of boots sit by the base of his dresser, and his small collection of clothes are hung in his closet by type and color. When he notices me looking, he pulls the sliding door completely closed.

"What exactly happened to you?" I ask.

"What do you mean, Ariana?"

"How did you end up in prison."

"I was convicted for possession and intent to distribute."

"No, I mean what happened to you? Not what you did. How did you end up getting mixed up in drugs? Nothing about your personality seems like you would make a decision like that."

"I needed the money."

He motions with his hand for me to take a seat. I sit as far away from him on the brown sofa as I can. His bed looks too neat to sit on.

"For what?"

"What kind of a question is that. I needed it for everything. I grew up in foster care. Then Jack. He always took care of the bills. I knew a lot but not enough. I lost my way. Got in way over my head. I was desperate to save the house which went into foreclosure but the vultures were circling. The bank wanted that property. They wanted to sell it for twice what it was worth. They didn't want me to save it and they succeeded. I didn't have any decent income or credit history. I barely got out of high school when he died."

"What about Jack's pension? The army has great benefits."

"You had to fill out a whole bunch of paperwork. Like I said. I was grieving. I was lost. I didn't do what I needed to do, and there wasn't anyone around to ask."

"That still doesn't seem like you."

"You don't know me like you think you do."

That seems like a loaded statement.

"I don't know everything about you, but I know enough. I know that you are an observer. You watch and assess and then only make a decision after you've examined the situation. Like right now. You're calculating something in your head about this conversation. I don't know whether you're leaving something out of your story or you just told me a complete boldface lie, but there's something. I just don't have any idea what it is."

"And how do you know that?"

"Your stormy gray eyes give you away every time."

Those eyes.

He stares at me with such intensity, I start to blush.

"You want to know what I'm thinking about right now?"

I shake my head silently.

He ignores me.

"What your hair looks like out of that ponytail you wear every day."

"I don't wear my hair out."

"Why?"

"I don't know. It's not practical for work."

"Take it out now," he commands.

I take a jittery sip of my tea.

"For what, I just—"

"I want to see if my assumption is correct."

"And what do you assume?"

"That you'll look even sexier with your hair out framing your gorgeous face."

"Stone."

I hold onto my mug tightly as he reaches over and behind my head to pull the black piece of elastic from around my hair. He watches with rapt attention as my auburn curls fall and bounce freely around my face.

When a genuine smile spreads across his face my head drops.

He has a killer smile which makes warmth spread from my cheeks straight to the rapidly swelling folds between my legs.

That's how I know I need to leave. If I stay one more minute in this room, I may not be a virgin in the morning.

TWENTY-EIGHT

STONE

I'm awestruck by her.

Not just because she's drop-dead gorgeous, that's a given, but because it's so fucking obvious that she doesn't know it. That's what makes her even more attractive.

She stands up to leave. To run. I'm not sure why she's so frightened. Maybe she can smell that I'm reeking of lust. That it's taking every ounce of self-control I have not to pick her up and toss her over on my bed.

"You should wear your hair like that more often."

"I told you, it's not practical."

"For work but work isn't everything, Ariana."

"Why do you always say my name like that."

"Like what?"

"Like I've never heard it before. Like I don't know that it's my name. Like you want to make sure that I understand how to pronounce it."

"It's your name."

"I'm well aware, Stone."

"It's a beautiful name."

She sighs as if she's exasperated.

"Take the compliment," I tell her.

"Thank you."

"It's the name your parents gave you. You should use it all the time."

"Your point?"

"I don't like your nickname."

"It's just a name. It doesn't mean anything."

"It's more than that to you and you know it."

"What are you psychoanalyzing me now, son of jack?"

I grab her hand.

"You're not that hard to figure out, daughter of Nate."

"Don't use my lines."

I chuckle.

She pulls her hand back gently.

"I think I should head upstairs now and crash. Good night, Stone."

"You watch *Supernatural*, right?" I blurt out.

She looks surprised by my observation.

I don't want her to leave.

"Sometimes."

"What season?"

"Are you saying that *you* watch *Supernatural*?" she asks incredulously.

"Sit down, Ariana."

"No, seriously."

"Yes, I watch *Supernatural*. Last time I remember I think I was on season four."

"Season four?" She chuckles. "Ha, I'm on season ten."

"Sit. Back. Down."

"I'm not watching season five all over again."

"Then we can do something else."

I grab around her waist and hold her steady in front of me, so that she can't run away.

"What would that be?" she asks softly.

With my hands around her diaphragm, I can feel her breaths quickening. That's how I already know the answer to the question before I ask it.

"Are you attracted to me, Ariana?"

"What...what are you asking me right now."

"I asked you a simple question. Are you attracted to me?"

"You're an attractive man, yes, but–"

"But what?"

"But nothing. I just...yes, you're attractive."

"I need more specifics."

I pull her down next to me and lift her legs across my lap. Then I start massaging her feet and calves.

"Specifically...does this make you feel good when I touch you?"

"I've had massages before, Stone, and yes I like them.

I work my hands farther up her legs, kneading her thighs.

She sucks in a deep inhalation of breath.

"Not a massage by me. What about here? Does this feel good?"

This is not a smart move. She's a virgin. Anything close to sexual that we do is only going to forge a stronger connection between us. One that I can't afford. But I've been thinking about doing this every night since I walked through the door, and my blue balls are the ones calling the shots right now, not my common sense.

Her body tenses up.

Then that damn dog on the other side of my door starts barking. I guess she senses Ariana's anxiety. I thought Bottle and I came to an agreement that I would sneak her extra jerky treats if she would stop treating me like an intruder. I guess something got lost in translation.

I look deep in Ariana's eyes so that she can understand me. Feel me.

"You don't ever have to be afraid of me, Ariana. I would never hurt you. Never."

"I'm not afraid."

"Uh huh...how about this then. Does this still feel good?"

My hands have moved closer between her legs. This is a no fly zone for me. Once I cross this line there's no going back. I have to live with this woman. I can't just wake up one day and pretend that it never happened. There can be no room for error on my part. But when her lips slightly part and she gasps ever so softly for me...that's when all of that shit goes out the window.

And I go for mine.

"How about now?" My voice descends lower. Thick with lust and desire.

Her eyes close as I begin to massage her pussy through her scrubs. All I feel is softness and steam heat. A heady mixture that makes me want to dive in and discover what she tastes like. It's been a very long time since I've tasted a woman.

Too long.

It used to be one of my favorite things to do. As far as I know, I was pretty damn good at it.

"Stone." She purrs my name in part angst and part pleasure.

"Ariana."

"I don't think we should."

"I didn't ask you to think. I asked you if you're attracted to me, and I asked you if it feels good. If you can't answer those two questions, then I don't want you to say another fucking thing."

I smile when I feel the increased wetness between her legs.

She likes this.

She needs this.

Just like I do.

She just needs a little gentle guidance to get her there.

"You're drenched," I growl.

Her legs tighten together. I've embarrassed her, and she's trying to keep me from further exploration, but an explorer won't be denied.

The satisfaction is totally in the journey.

TINY

"What's wrong, Ariana."

I'm scared to death which is why I'm the last virgin left on the planet earth.

"Ummm, my father could come in any second."

So lame.

"Your father isn't coming home any time soon. He's on a date with Savannah's mother, although they're calling it some other shit to pretend that that's not what it is. And even if he comes home, the door to this room is locked, and we're consenting adults."

"I know, it's just weird."

"I'm going to make it not weird. I'm going to make it so that you're not going to give a flying fuck who's in this house."

"Where is this coming from?" I ask.

"What."

"You, me, this. You wanting me like this? I thought–"

"You thought wrong. *This* right here has been coming since the moment I walked behind your big beautiful ass up those steps. You telling me that your surprised by that. That you had no idea that I've been wanting to get my hand in between those thighs for weeks."

This man.

He just says whatever he feels like.

"To be honest, yes."

"Stand up."

"What?"

He swings my legs off of his lap.

"Stand up and stand directly in front of me."

I feel utterly ridiculous. I can't maintain eye contact with him. My hands are jittery. I don't think that I can do this. Not because I'm some sort of conservative prude that's waiting to hold onto my virginity for marriage, but because I don't know what the hell I'm doing. He's probably been fucking for half of his life and hasn't had a woman in years thanks to jail, and so now he wants to sleep with me of all people? That's way too much pressure. I'll never live up to his standards.

"That's good, baby. Now look at me."

I struggle to look at him, but when he spreads his legs and pulls me in closer to him by my waist, I feel a little more at ease. He doesn't say anything for a moment but just holds me. My breathing slows. I relax a bit more.

"Look at me," he demands. "I'm going to ask you this one last time. Are. You. Attracted. To. Me. Yes or no?"

"Yes," I exhale bravely.

"Does it feel good to you when I touch you? Yes or no?"

It takes me a moment but then I finally answer realizing what he needs from me. Why he's taking his time. He needs me to give him the words. To tell him that it's okay. So, I give him what we both need.

"Yes."

"Thank fuck. That's the right answer, baby."

He slowly slides my pants to the floor.

"Step out of them," he demands.

Other than my panties, I'm unclothed from the waist down, and he's seated low on the sofa directly in line with my sex. I'm wearing a pair of butter yellow thongs which he aggressively tears apart with his bare hands. As the frilly fabric falls from my body I hear something tantamount to a growl come deep from within his chest.

He rubs and kneads my ass cheeks while kissing me gently on the navel, below my navel, and all over my thighs.

"I love this ass." He presses the words into my skin and my head falls to the side in bliss.

He uses his thumbs to gently pull apart the swollen folds of my labia and begins to lick. Soft laps at first. Then they grow hungrier. More desperate.

"I knew you'd taste this fucking sweet, Ariana."

I break out in a thin layer of sweat as the powerful sensations of his tongue massage me into a bliss that I've never known before. He palms the back of my ass with an even firmer grasp and pulls me in closer. Devouring me almost body and soul.

Then he starts to move his head in a back and forth motion, turning his tongue into a human vibrator, and I feel my knees about to give from under me. I fall forward, grabbing onto the sides of his head and hold on for dear life.

"Stone!" I cry out for him to stop or keep going. I'm not sure which.

"This is a good pussy," he damn near grunts with his mouth directly on my clit.

"I'm going to come."

My whole body is coiling and winding and building. I can feel energy coursing through my veins and pumping oxygen rich blood to my heart and my lungs.

"No, you're not," he tells me. "You're not going to come until I tell you to come."

Is he insane?

"But Stone–"

"Not until I give you permission. Now spread wider. You're closing up on me."

"I can't!" I exclaim breathlessly.

Bottle starts to scrape at the bottom of the door. Trying to get in. *Great timing, girl.* She thinks I'm in trouble.

Yeah, girl, I'm in big trouble.

I'm about to come and scream bloody murder in one damn minute, and then the whole block is going to think I'm in trouble.

THIRTY

STONE

I pull my face completely away from Ariana's heavenly pussy, and trust me when I say it hurts me more than it does her, but this is how I like to play.

Her eyes are dazed for a moment.

Glassy.

Good.

I allow her a moment to come down. Away from the cliff. Her breathing slows a bit just when I think it's almost back to normal, I dive greedily back in. Pulling her forward and guiding her to a straddle position of my face on the couch. Now I can really lie back and get my shit off. This is the perfect position.

Her moans come faster and grow louder as I continue thoroughly eating her out.

"Is this my pussy now?" I demand to know.

She doesn't respond.

Well she kind of does with cries of satisfaction, but I need actual human words. Talking dirty is probably new to her, and I get that, but ignorance is not an excuse. So, I'll keep asking until I get the answers I require.

"Is this shit mine, Ariana. I'm going to need the words, baby."

I smack one of her ass cheeks with a full spread out palm.

"Yeeeess," she manages to yelp. Falling farther forward with her palms against the wall above my head.

I'm as hard as a titanium baseball bat, but I'm getting so much gratification out of giving Ariana pleasure that it doesn't matter. I'd walk around for a week with this boner if I can get her off. She makes me feel like a god.

"Can I come yet, Stone?"

Look at my baby. Already using her manners.

I can't deny her anything.

"Yes, baby. Come for me."

Then I take one hard pull on her clit and smack her other ass cheek and she blows for me.

"Stone!" she cries. I love hearing her come with my name on her lips.

She continues to shudder with numerous aftershocks as I lick all the cream from her pussy. Savoring every drop. I would probably start all over again if I wasn't so anxious to get inside of her.

"Every single moment of that was worth waiting five years for," I tell her.

She's still breathing heavily. Coming down off of her orgasmic high.

I lift her up in my arms and she wraps her legs around my waist.

I take a seat on the bed and sit her on my lap. Staring her straight in the eyes. Not giving her even a second to shut down on me.

"You were amazing, baby. You look absolutely beautiful when you come. Did you know that?"

"No."

"Well you do and now I'm going to make you come again. This time with me inside of you. Do you want that?"

She shakes her head.

"The words, Ariana."

"I want you inside of me. I want you to be my first."

And her last if I have anything to say about it.

"Take off your top."

Still sitting on my lap, I hold onto her by her hips. Making sure she doesn't fall. Reinforcing the fact that I've got her. That she's safe. I love that she is the perfect size for me. I don't feel as if I'm going to break her. We both have something strong and solid to hold onto. Each other.

She's wearing a yellow bra that matches the thong I destroyed. It clasps in the front and when she releases it, her breasts spring forward as if they've been released from a terrible life of bondage.

I see various indents and lines in her soft skin from where the bra was holding her in, and I start tracing those lines with my tongue. Soothing the angry marks until she wraps her arms around my neck.

I look up into her eyes and know that I am forever marked. She is mine now. We are an us, and I'm going to have a shit load of work to do to protect it. But I'll worry about all of that later. For now, I need to claim what's mine.

I bend down and gently kiss her on the mouth. Sliding my tongue partly inside so that she is sure to get a bit of a taste of herself. Her tongue hesitantly but gradually begins to fall into a rhythm with mine until I finally pull away.

Licking my top lip after I'm done.

It was one hell of a kiss.

The type of kiss you feel deep inside of your balls.

The kind of kiss that has me wanting to spill my guts before I steal her virginity.

That maybe I should tell her that I'm in trouble. Confide in her the truth of what's going on. Ask her to help me get into that safe. Maybe I could trust her. Maybe she could trust me. Maybe then I could touch her without feeling like a complete hypocrite when I do.

Then again...maybe she'd get up, walk out of this room, and never come back.

I'm such a selfish asshole.

I should stop.

"Make love to me, Stone."

Fuck me.

"I want it to be you."

I squeeze my eyes tightly and call on every bit of self-discipline I have. It doesn't work. I want her too much. I need her too much. I'll tell her the truth later. Make her understand later. Right now, I need to give her what we both need. It would be cruel to deny us that.

I start kissing her neck.

Then she pulls gently back and lifts up my shirt.

I turn us around and lay her on the bed. Staring at her like a hungry wolf while I push down and step out of my sweats and boxer briefs.

Her eyes reactively bulge when she first stares at my dick. Probably a little afraid of its size and girth. She actually should be. I'm a big boy, but I'm counting on the fact that she doesn't have much to compare it to. So, I'm not going to make a big deal out of it if she doesn't.

Ariana has exquisite breasts.

Full mounds with large caramel colored areolas and nipples.

She squirms as I wrap my hand around the left one and

squeeze gently. Popping the nipple into my mouth as I pinch and pull the nipple of the right.

"Play with yourself," I order with a mouth full of nipple.

I continue my own play as I watch her as she explores herself. She slides her finger gingerly around her clit. Grinding her own hips upward to meet the movement of her finger. It's beautiful to watch and it makes my cock ache with more need than I've ever felt before.

"It's my turn," I say gruffly.

I knock her hand away and start playing with her pussy myself. Sliding one then two of my fingers inside. I pump them slowly in and out and watch as she continues to rock her pelvis up and down. Basically, fucking my fingers.

"That's good, baby. You're getting ready for me. That's all you're going to need to do when I get in side of you. Pump your pussy like you're doing right now."

She moves even faster.

Ariana definitely likes it when I talk to her.

"Can you even pump faster, baby? Show me."

She fucks my fingers even faster and I can feel her creaming all over them. I slide one more in. Getting her good and ready.

Her mouth starts to part and she's panting now. Pumping and panting. I need to slow her down if I want her to come with me inside of her.

"Please, Stone," she begs. And so there goes that plan. I've got to give her what she needs. I continue to pump and slide my thumb over her clit a couple of times.

"Stone...please," she begs again. Making me damn near want to cry myself.

I pull my fingers out and give her pussy a good whack with my hand.

And she explodes.

Her back and body arches in orgasmic bliss.

And like a good dog does to its master, I make sure to lick her completely clean.

<<<<>>>>

THIRTY-ONE

TINY

I am literally seeing stars. Millions and millions of little floating stars are bouncing around the periphery of my vision. There's a medical terminology for what this actual phenomena is, which I learned in nursing school, but I forget what it is. For now, I'm going to call it what it is.

A great fucking orgasm.

I've come before. I've even had oral sex before, but I've never felt anything like this. Now I understand why some women lose their minds. This feeling, this euphoria, can probably become...addictive.

As my body floats down from this beautiful extraterrestrial place, I can see Stone out of the corner of my eye. He's standing by the bed, with a wide grin on his face, sliding a condom on the biggest dick I've ever seen in my life. Not that I have many to compare it to.

He climbs back on the bed and starts kissing my breasts. This is it. Some kind of way we're going to defy all the laws of science and he's going push that big engorged piece of muscle into my narrow vaginal cavity.

Relax, nut ball.

Women do this shit every day.

"Relax, baby. This is going to feel even better than what we just did."

Is that even possible?

When Stone hovers his big, beautiful body above me I drink him in. The detailed tattoo of an American eagle on his chest. The small heart and anchor on his neck. I wrap my arms around his body and run my hands up and down his back.

I hate to think it. It's such a frightening admission. But I want this man.

I want him like I've never wanted anything in my life.

And I'm about to have him.

"Get out of your head, Ariana, and focus on me. Keep your eyes on me."

I do as I'm told and stare into a pair of expressive gray eyes that are trying to tell me all of the things that the man who owns them cannot say himself.

He cares for me.

He wants to protect me.

He wants to ravage me.

He wants to own me.

He positions the tip of his penis directly at the entrance of my sex and starts to push and pull. Creating a gentle rhythm with his hips.

"Remember what you did when my fingers were inside of you, baby. Do the same thing."

Push and pull.

Lift and lower.

Pump in and out.

We continue this delicate dance of give and take as he continues to slide farther and farther inside of me until we reach an impasse.

He wraps one of his massive hands around the base of my neck and stares hungrily into my eyes.

"Your ass, this pussy, all of you belongs to me now."

"I know."

"And this dick moving inside of you, belongs to you."

And before I can respond he pushes past the thin barrier and farther inside of me. I claw his back as he continues and in a matter of moments I understand what I'm supposed to do. My hips rise and fall to meet his continued thrusts, and we build a sweet momentum that evolves into a frenzied passion and finally into an agonizing free fall.

I come yet again.

With Stone inside of me.

Howling an indescribable goodbye prayer to the virgin goddesses.

And slightly embarrassed that I might just have blown out Stone's eardrums.

THIRTY-TWO

TINY

JUNE

I am in the middle of a sexual revolution. I mean I am really feeling myself. Stone and I are fucking like bunnies, and I think the excitement around it is even heightened because he's reluctantly agreed to keep it a secret from my father for now.

We have had sex in his room seven times. Eight if you count the time he just ate me out.

My room twice.

The shower three times. Which was awwwwwesome.

He's visited me at the hospital, and we actually did it in a vacant hospital room. Okay, that was crazy. I won't be doing that again.

We would have done it at the bike shop but Savannah is always hovering around aka cock blocking. So, I just bring him dinner there sometimes or lunch if I'm off work.

It's been wonderful. I don't know what took me so long to finally do this. Or maybe it's just that I had to wait for the right person.

"Hey, baby."

"Shh," I say quietly. "Or Savannah might hear you."

"Who gives a shit."

"My father will."

"Have you ever considered the possibility that your father would be happy for us."

"Umm, no."

"And why is that."

"He doesn't think anyone is good enough for me. It's probably part of why it took me so long to give up the goods."

"Then I appreciate him even more."

I smack him on his arm.

"Shut up."

"Your parents seemed like they were really in love. I would think that he'd want that for you."

"Are you saying that you love me?" I ask in jest.

"I don't know, Ariana. Are we in love?" he asks with one of his poker faces.

I'm not sure if he's playing or serious, and I'm not going to even touch that loaded question with a ten-foot pole. I just start laying out the dinner that I've brought him. Rosemary chicken and garlic mashed potatoes. One of his favorite meals.

"My parents were madly in love. Why do you think he can't let go of her? I'm not sure I even want to be in that type of love. I think it pains him every day to live in this world without her."

"He's dating though."

"Barely. Savannah's mother is not my mother."

"Tell me about your mother," he says as he sits down at the table that's always been too small for him to sit at.

"Well, she was a beauty. A great cook. She was actually

a caterer. She always had dreams of working in the medical profession though. I think if she had been born later or to more affluent parents she would have been a doctor."

"How did she die?"

"She was in a freak accident. Her car was paralleled parked on a busy road, and she was sideswiped by a tractor trailer when she was getting inside."

"I'm sorry, babe. That's terrible."

"I was young. There was a closed casket and then she was cremated. I didn't get to see her. It was just bad."

"Where was she from?"

"Around the Drexel University area before gentrification. Working class folks who did their best but couldn't afford to send her to college. As legend tells it she was a real beauty in her neighborhood. All the guys pursued her. In fact, I think my father stole her from her longtime boyfriend."

"Yeah? Like I stole you from Bill and Jake and—"

"Quiet." I roll my eyes. "You're so bad."

"I want to be even naughtier if you give me the thumbs-up. I'll slide all of this shit off the table and give it to you right and proper. I'll lean you over the table, while you hold onto the edge, and I'll fuck you from the back. You'll love that, baby."

That sounds sooo good, but I can't risk it. Not here. Maybe I'll remind him when we're home.

"Shhh." I laugh. "She's going to hear you."

"Fine, okay. So Nate stole your mama away from her poor old boyfriend, and then they lived happily ever after?"

"Pretty much except I think my mom always felt a little bad about it. The whole family thought she was going to marry Silas. They didn't really know my dad yet, so I think they gave him a hard way to go at first."

Stone's face drops.

"Did you say Silas?"

"Yeah."

"Same age as your dad?"

"I don't know, probably. They were in the army around the same time. It's possible your dad knew him too."

"Holy shit."

"What?!"

"This is a vendetta."

"What's a vendetta?"

"I need to tell you something, Ariana, and you're not going to like it."

"Then I don't want to hear it."

"Ariana."

I drop to my knees and start unbuckling Stone's jeans. Giving killer fellatio is one of the skills I've been perfecting over the last few weeks, and Stone has enjoyed every teaching moment.

"Ariana—" he offers a weak plea for me to stop when in actuality he really wants me to keep going. "Fuck."

His eyes roll back in his head.

I'm so happy right now. For once I don't feel smothered or suffocated. I feel like I can breathe. I'm not ready for the world to come crashing around me.

He grips my hair tightly right before he comes with a muffled roar. Doing his best to keep Savannah from figuring out what we're doing back here, although I'm pretty sure that the gig is up.

I look up at him with a wide-eyed grin as I wipe my mouth.

"I love you," he tells me and for the first time I think I see it. Genuine emotion in his eyes. He might just love me. So, I dive into the deep end of the water too.

"I love you too."

"Let's close out the books and go home."

"And what are we going to do when we get there?"

"I'm going to teach you how to ride my cock reverse cowboy style. You're going to love that one."

Viva La Revolution!

THIRTY-THREE

STONE

This is going to be the hardest conversation I've ever had to have, but I've put it off for as long as I could. I just wanted a few more days of Ariana and Nate looking at me like the man I desperately want to be, and not the man I really am–a thief, a liar, or a bastard.

Part of the reason why I'm a felon, why my life has turned out like this, is because I've always believed that I've had to go it alone. I was alone as a baby. Alone in school. Alone in foster care. And after Jack died, I was alone again.

It never dawned on me to ask for help. It wasn't something I'd ever been used to doing, but I have to do things differently if I expect different results. Jack taught me that. I have to trust someone for once. I have to ask for help. And it starts tonight.

"First, I want to say that I truly appreciate you taking me into your home, Nate. You have been more than gracious. Both you and Ariana."

"Of course, son. It's been a pleasure having you."

"With that said, this is going to be hard for me to say, but I've been lying to you. To both of you for some time."

I watch closely as his face drops.

"What is it, Stone. I'll help you if I can."

"I ask that you give me a second to explain everything in its entirety before you write me off."

"Go ahead and say your piece."

"Jack was a great father to me, but he had his demons. He gambled a lot. Bought women a lot. When he died he had a lot of debts and not much income. I'm sure there was some sort of death benefit pension payout I could have gotten from the army when he died, but I didn't know anything about it at the time, and I didn't think to ask for help. I didn't think anyone would help me."

"I'm sorry about that, Stone. I know I got defensive the last time we talked about this, but I should've done a better job of making sure you were okay. I'm sure Jack would have done the same for Ariana if the roles were reversed."

"Maybe...but anyway I was lost and lonely and angry, and I channeled all of that rage into some very dangerous habits. One of them was robbing drug dealers. Heroin dealers to be specific. I blamed them for ruining my life. So I targeted them. I'd rob them of a shipment, and dump it in the Hudson River."

Nate doesn't move a muscle.

In fact, he doesn't say a word.

Almost as if he knows where this conversation is headed.

To a place he wants no parts of.

"To earn money to live, and I was living well, I would shake down some of the smaller dealers, but my goal was to completely debilitate the heroin supply chain in my part of Brooklyn. Obviously, that was a bit ambitious. I made some mistakes. The biggest one being that I got caught holding a large amount of product. Now that I look back on it, I probably was set up.

"As you already know I was charged with possession and intent to sell, and I received a seven year sentence for it. Since I got pinched, the dealer I stole from knew how to find me. The smack I stole from him was worth seven million dollars on the street. He paid me a visit in prison. The dealer's goes by the name Bucky. His real name is Silas."

I wait for a reaction from Nate, but he still doesn't say a word, although his face grows harder and harder. Is he actually going to make me say it?

"And evidently he had partners. One of them supposedly being Jack."

"Your father."

"Yes."

"You would have known if your father was a drug dealer."

"You would think that wouldn't you, but I guess Jack had his demons like everyone else. Maybe he had a good reason for doing it at the time. I don't know. I guess I'll never know. Anyway, I'm telling you all this because this Silas person is blackmailing me."

"What does he want?"

"He wants his money or he wants me to hurt you or he wants me to die."

Nate stands up.

"Hurt me?"

"Yes, one of the choices was to get close to Ariana and then break her. The point being that he wants to destroy you, Nate. You are the other partner that he claims stole something precious from him. Something like the love of his life."

"Why would you involve us in this, Stone," he says with an icy glare that I never even thought he was capable of. "Why would you put my daughter at risk like this."

"Let's not play these games anymore, Nate. I'm telling you first before I tell Ariana."

"Tell her the fuck what exactly."

"Do you have seven million dollars in that vault?"

"Well that's my fucking business isn't it."

"Were you and Jack partners with Silas."

"Again, not your business."

"He's going to kill me, Nate. Do you give two shits about me?"

"Do I give two shits? You came into my home, putting my daughter in harm's way, all to save your thieving ass."

"Or maybe you're the one putting Ariana at risk. Those three dudes who robbed the store knew you had a safe. They knew that there was something of value in it. They didn't just randomly pick a fucking Harley dealership. How do they know, Nate? You still selling drugs?"

"No, but I think you're on drugs."

"How did you pay for Penn."

"With grit and hard work."

"How did you write that university a check every year when your business barely clears enough profit to pay your fucking mortgage?"

"What do you want from me?"

"I want you to save my life! That's what I want."

"If I give you the seven million dollars you will have to walk away from Ariana."

"What."

"I'm not stupid. I know the two of you have been seeing each other. I also know that if she is keeping it a secret from me that you're already in her head. Changing her.

Corrupting her. I won't have it. She is best thing I ever did. The purest thing I have left from a messy life. I won't have her destroyed by someone lost like you. If I give you the money. You walk away. That's the deal."

"Lost like me?"

"You go around doing these ridiculously stupid things, taking these huge risks, because you think the world owes you something. You think drugs or drug dealers destroyed your life because your mother was an addict. Guess what not only does the world not owe you anything, but that whole entire story was just a lie that the social workers told you, and that Jack allowed you to believe.

"Your biological parents didn't want you. There's no horrible story why. There's no system to blame. They fucked-up and they didn't want to take responsibility for their mistake. In case you want to go looking for them, your last name is King and you were born here in Philadelphia. Not New York. So there you have it. The long lost son is home again. Leave here and find your way, but leave my child out of it."

Nate just mind fucked me.

But there's one thing I will continually be sure of and those are my feelings for Ariana. I love her, and there's no deal to be made when it comes to that.

"No deal, motherfucker."

I whip open the door to storm out and find the last person on earth I hoped would be on the other side.

She was supposed to be at work.

And there are tears running down her grief-stricken face.

THIRTY-FOUR

STONE

JULY

I'm sitting on the stone ledge of a massive ornate fountain that stands across from Memorial Hospital. It's a sweltering Philadelphia summer day, and I'm eating a cherry water ice, while random droplets of water from the fountain hit the back of my neck. Temporarily cooling me down.

I'm waiting for her.

It's become a ritual lately.

It's actually kind of pathetic that it's come to this. Skulking around in parks or across streets, but I need to do this. Sometimes I get a glimpse of her when she goes out for lunch. Sometimes I catch a peek after work. Once in a while she's with the asshole doctor from the juice bar, but I don't even let that bother me. I just need to put eyes on her, and I'll take it any way that I can get it.

Just because I fucked-up doesn't mean I'm ever going to stop looking out for what's mine. And make no mistake about it–Ariana Carter is mine. She'll always be mine. I just wished she agreed.

Unfortunately, the night that I confronted Nate, Ariana overheard at least fifty percent of that conversation. That wasn't how I planned for her to find out. She knows that I've been lying to her for months. She knows that I've been sneaking behind their backs looking for money. Money that I planned on taking. She knows that Nate said he'd give it to me if I just left and never looked back.

But she doesn't know everything. At least I don't think she does. He has yet to admit that he was a heroin trafficker back in the day, and that he fell in love with the girlfriend of one of his partners. But even if she did hear parts of that, I suppose it doesn't matter.

That wasn't why her face was contorted into ugly tears when I opened that door and found her there.

It wasn't why she threw the few items of clothing I own out in the street.

It wasn't why Bottle growled and bit my calf as I desperately tried to plead my case.

It wasn't why she changed her number, so that now when I call her cell phone, all I get is a man with a thick Taiwanese accent.

God, I fucked-up.

I can barely remember her voice anymore.

"You stick out here like a sore thumb. If you're trying to be inconspicuous you aren't doing a good job. You're big as shit."

It's Bucky.

As I figured, six months on the nose, he's found me.

Ready to collect.

And like the idiot I am, I'm within six feet of Ariana. Putting her in danger yet again. When will I learn.

"You stick out as well," I counter. "With that hot-ass suit on in ninety-degree weather and that godawful pirate patch. Why don't you wear a pair of glasses like Stevie Wonder or Ray Charles? Have some class.

"This is a war injury, thank you very much, and I'm not blind. Wearing this patch is like wearing a badge of honor."

"An honor for pirates everywhere."

Bucky sits down next to me. I can tell that my words have annoyed him which will probably be the highlight of my day.

"I'm dying to see how things have panned out. Do you have my money?"

"No."

"Aww, that's unfortunate. I was actually routing for you. With the balls on you, I thought you might have figured something out, *but* I guess that left you with option number two. Were you able to make Miss Carter fall in love with you?"

"Yes."

A slimy grins spreads across his face.

"And did you break her?"

"Yes."

"Then why are you sitting outside of her place of employment like a lovesick puppy?" *Because I am.* "Getting back together with her was not part of the deal. You're not supposed to be putting her pieces back together. Honestly, if you did your job right she shouldn't even be at work."

"I'm not getting back together with her."

"This is low, even for you, Silas."

We both turn our heads at the sound of Nate's voice. He walked up behind us on the other side of the fountain. I must stink at this inconspicuous shit, because both he and

Bucky found me. They knew right where I'd be. Wherever she is.

"Nate."

Bucky stands even though Nate still towers over him by at least five or six inches.

"Why are you at my daughter's job, Silas?"

"Following him." He points to me chuckling. "How does it feel to know that the man you brought into your home broke your daughter's heart? Bet it doesn't feel good, does it?"

"You are ruining my daughter's life over her mother? Joanne never loved you, Silas. You have to know that. You were a childhood boyfriend. I was the love of her life."

"You and I were friends. Rangers. Brothers. I introduced you to her! You ate food in my house with us. You partied with us. You betrayed me in the worst way, Nate, and you fucking know it. Just admit it."

"I admitted it a hundred years ago."

"Then you got her pregnant."

"I apologized to you."

"Then you married her."

"I loved her!"

"As did I, you sanctimonious motherfucker."

A few people at the fountain start to walk away as Nate and Bucky's voices rise higher.

"I was willing to change for her. You weren't. I turned my life around. I stopped all that bullshit we were doing, and ran my grandfather's shop for the last twenty-five years, because that's the type of man she deserved."

"She deserved more."

"She was happy until the day she died."

"Says you."

I'm so engrossed in watching these two old grumps hash

out their love vendetta, that I totally miss the fact that Ariana has spotted us and started walking toward us. It throws me at first, because she isn't dressed in scrubs. She's in regular clothing. A black pencil skirt, a light blue dressy tank and black pumps. She looks fucking amazing.

I walk toward her as Nate and Bucky continue their spat. My deadened heart starts to beat. Blood starts to pump into my dick again. My body is coming alive. I'm drawn to her like a thirsty man toward a cool, clean mountain spring.

"Ariana."

THIRTY-FIVE

STONE

I fight the urge to wrap my hands around her body.

"What is going on over there?" she asks with a purely professional tone to her voice.

"Nate and Bucky, I mean Silas, are hashing a few things out."

Her eyes widen.

"That's him?"

"Yes."

"Is he here for you?"

"Yes."

"Is he going to kill you?" her lip quivers for just a second.

"No, baby."

"How do you know that for sure?"

"Because I assured him that I broke you. It was his contingency plan just in case I couldn't find the money."

"Was I such an easy mark? Did I look that desperate to you both that you thought you could easily seduce me then hurt me?" she asks angrily.

"No, Ariana."

"I guess it was easy though, wasn't it? You completed your *mission,* convict. You broke the virgin. Kudos to you."

Her words are caustic and hurt me with a marksman's precision.

"That wasn't my mission. Drug money was the mission. Falling in love with you was an unexpected fork in the road. I was never going to do what Bucky asked. Even if I hadn't found the money. I was never going to intentionally hurt you. Like you said, I didn't even know if I could."

She looks over at Bucky.

"He hates me and my father that much that he'd rather destroy me than get his seven million dollars back? That makes no sense."

"I think he knew that I'd never be able to get the money. He was counting on it. This was all about hurting the one thing Nate loves above all else and that was you."

"Then he should be satisfied, because you definitely did hurt me. I'm broken beyond repair. That's why I'm leaving. To put the pieces back together."

My chest fills with dread.

"Where are you going?"

"Rhode Island."

"What's in Rhode Island."

"Not you. Not my father. A new job. A fresh start. A man I can trust."

"What the fuck are you talking about, Ariana. What man?"

She smiles, but it's not a genuine smile, it's the kind you make right before you go in for a pleasurable kill.

"The one good thing to come out of this is that you taught me well, and now I'm a pretty good lay. I plan on fine tuning those skills with Bill. I'll have plenty of time for fucking since my job is practically half the hours and double the pay. It's a sweet gig. Be happy for me, son of Jack."

She's purposely trying to fuck with me and it's working.

My normal reaction would be to slide my mask back down.

Or shake the shit out of her.

But I'm not going to do either.

I'm going to show her who I really am.

A man who's in love with her.

"Don't do this."

"Don't do what? Be happy?"

"I can make you happy." I walk up closer to her. "I will spend my life making sure of it."

"I'm leaving. It's done."

I vigorously rub my hand up and down my face. This being a better man shit is hard. I'm desperately looking for the right words. Words that will make her see.

"Nothing is done. You are right here. Standing in front of me, and I'm telling you that I love you. That I will keep loving you. That I will become the better man that you deserve. The man your father became for your mother. We will have that kind of love."

Heavy tears start to fall from Ariana's eyes.

I walk just a bit closer to her.

I wipe one of her tears with my thumb then lick it off.

"I will swallow all of your tears if you let me, baby."

"You've never talked this much in your entire life."

"I'm an eloquent motherfucker when I want to be."

I move in closer.

Dwarfing her sweet curves with my body.

"Don't leave me, Ariana."

I slide one of my hands against the side of her face and

into her hair. Pulling it gently, so her head can naturally tilt back and her eyes can fall into mine.

"Stone."

"I love you."

"I don't love you," she whispers.

"You're lying."

"I hate you."

"I can fuck all that hate right out of you."

She starts to pull away.

Maybe I should talk about fucking later.

"I will die for you!" I blurt out.

Her arms slowly encircle my waist.

"I don't want you to die."

"Do you want me to live?"

"Yes."

"Then never talk about leaving me again."

I'm not sure when they left, but I notice that Nate and Bucky have disappeared. That can't be good, but it doesn't matter right now. I have to talk some sense into my girl. I think I'm breaking through.

"Everything is a mess."

She falls into my arms.

"Life is complicated," I say in her ear. "But I've learned a big lesson since I've met you. Things are not always black and white. Life is full of grays. Your father is not the villain and neither really is Bucky. We will work it out."

"But Silas—"

"Is not going to kill me. I know that finally for the first time today. If he was going to do it, he would have done it by now."

She squeezes me tighter.

It feels like home.

"I missed you, Stone."

"Not as much as I missed you. I've been lost without you. You're my north star, baby. Without you I'm totally adrift."

She reaches up and pulls my head down to hers.

Our foreheads meet.

Then I move in for a kiss.

Sliding my tongue home where it belongs. Home. Inside of her masterful mouth. When we break for a breath, she giggles.

"You've been reading some of my books, haven't you?"

"Uh-uh," I lie. "I don't read."

"The hell you don't. When I threw you out of the house, I think you stole some of my books. That line is from a novel I read about three months ago."

"Could be."

"You don't have to borrow other people's words, Stone. You talk to me in all the ways that matter. Better than any character in my romances ever could."

"Then let me take you somewhere where I can talk to you in every way that fucking matters. I've got a lot to say."

THIRTY-SIX

TINY

AUGUST

We stumble into Stone's small hotel room on 13th Street. The place we've been making love and that he's been living in ever since I threw him out.

I'll never understand it, but thanks to his new relationship with crazy ass Jake and The Chosen Riders, he's been able to earn money repairing and restoring many of their bikes. In fact, they've worked out a deal where he is on the club payroll and can use one of their safe house addresses to show his parole officer.

He said that he will never return to the shop, even though I told him how my father ended up giving Silas the money to settle his debt. It wasn't close to seven million dollars, but it was a substantial amount. Enough to send him on his way and leave us alone. But like Stone said, maybe it was never about the money. Maybe he just wanted to rattle my father's cage.

I laugh when I trip and fall over a pair of Stone's size thirteen work boots. He hikes up my skirt and lifts me up on the slick wooden desk in the room.

"Guess what I got," I say as he pretty much yanks off my top and rips open my bra.

"A good pussy."

"No...guess again."

"Spread your legs," he growls.

"The City of Philadelphia sent me a check for five thousand dollars."

"For what?"

He slides my butt forward and slides one of his beefy fingers inside of me.

"The partial strip search the police officers did when they arrested me was illegal. I was automatically included in a class action suit someone filed and that was the payout!"

"Nice."

He slides another finger inside of me, probably because he thinks I'm talking too much. That one does the trick. I shut up and start clawing at his shoulders.

"Did they search you like this, baby?"

"No," I groan in ecstasy.

He lifts me off the desk, turns me over, and hikes up my skirt even farther.

"Hold onto the desk."

"The lamp is in—"

He slides everything that was on the desk onto the floor. It all falls to the carpeted floor with a thud. Then he smacks one of my ass cheeks.

"Spread your legs wider."

He lines himself up at my entrance and begins to push his way inside. This position is still very new for me, so I'm tight and tense, but the feeling of him hitting me from the back is starting to feel like my new favorite position.

He fucks me fast and hard.

We both come quickly.

Panting from the intensity of our orgasms.

He pulls out of me and carries me to the bed. He sits on the edge and pulls me on top, so that I am straddling him.

"I love you," he says matter of factly.

"I love you too."

I kiss his eyelids, then massage his freshly shorn head. This man makes me so happy.

"What are you going to do with all your extra cash?" he asks practically purring from the massage I'm giving him.

"It's gone."

"What did you spend it on already, greedy girl."

"Our new apartment."

"Our what?"

"I realize that I was suffocating myself. Making myself miserable. All I had to do was leave, so that's what I'm doing. I'll miss taking care of my father, and I'll miss Bottle too, but they will be fine. They have each other. Just like you and I have each other. I want us to live together. I mean...if that's what you want."

"You're going to need to get your money back, Ariana."

My stomach drops.

"What?"

I thought we were on the same page, but I guess we weren't. I try wiggling off of his lap, but he holds me in place by wrapping his thick, tattooed arms around me.

"Everything I'd been told about my birth family was a lie. Jack paid off workers at the agency to make sure that the lie continued."

"Why?"

"I guess Jack didn't want me to go looking for them. Like many adoptive parents, I think he was frightened. I'll never be sure of why, but what I do know is that I was born out of inconvenience, not addiction and hopelessness. I have living, breathing family members, and some of them were looking for me."

"That's fantastic, Stone!"

"I didn't want to tell you until I met with them. Made sure that it was real. My father is dead and I'm not sure who my mother is, but I know that I have two brothers. I like them, babe. And you should see them. I look just like them."

"Wow."

"They said that all the things that I'm good at are all the very attributes that will work well in the *family business*."

"They want you to work with them?"

"Yeah and I think I'm going to do it."

"So that's why you don't want to live with me?"

"Babe, they're fucking loaded. I'm going to be making three times what you do. I'm not trying to rain on your independent woman parade, but we're going to need a bigger place."

"Ohhhh."

"I can't wait for you to meet them."

"I can't believe that there's actually two other men in the world who look like you. What are their names?"

"Camden and Cutter."

"King?"

"Yeah, how'd you know that?"

"Oh, holy shit. I know them. Well I sort of know them. We have mutual friends. My friend Sloan is seeing your brother, Cutter. And yes...I can see the resemblance."

"Damn, what are the chances. Of course, I'm the better looking brother, right? I am the oldest."

He nuzzles his face in the crook of my neck.

"When they made you, honey, they broke the mold. Those boys are only cheap imitations."

"That, Ariana Carter, deserves a reward from your teacher. I'm going to fuck you right and proper in the shower, and then we'll pick up where we left off with *Supernatural*. Season five, episode one."

Not ready to let go of these hot brothers? I wasn't either:) Read more King Brother drama, hotness, and happily ever afters in their sexy novella Promised To A King.

Somebody's getting married y'all!

"I love that we get a little more of the Kings!"
-ARC Reviewer

Read this King family update now.

LISA LANG BLAKENEY

DOWNLOAD PROMISED INSTANTLY!
Also Available On Audio

BONUS STUFF!

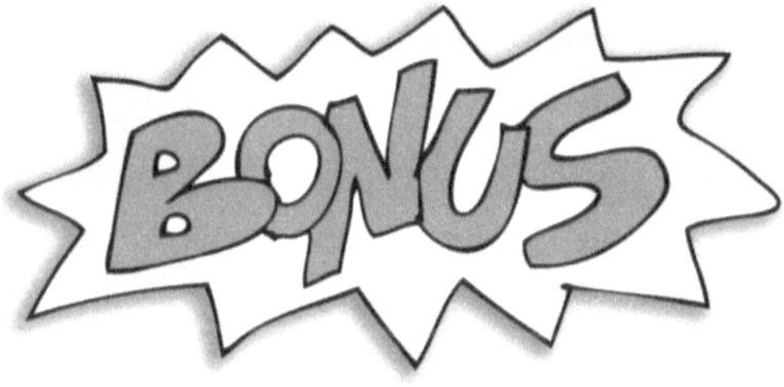

Want access to all my bonus stuff? Read deleted scenes, character interviews, and extended epilogues for all of my releases when you visit the **Romance Ninja Room**.

CLICK FOR EXCLUSIVE ACCESS
http://lisalangblakeney.com/private-ninja-room/

WHERE YOU CAN FIND ME

1. I have a VIP mailing list. I only send free books, new release, sale or special giveaway information to this group. No spam. You can join here: http://LisaLangBlakeney.com/VIP .

2. I have a private Fan & Readers Group also known as my "Ninjas" a.k.a. "Alpha Romance Warriors" where I share all things new going on, teasers, yummy pics, and just chit chat. It's a closed group for ages 18+ and over, and what we post won't show on your public feed: https://www.facebook.com/groups/romanceninjas/

3. I have a special ARC team. If you enjoy my books and would like a free advanced reader copy of my next book in exchange for an honest review on release day, then feel free to apply. There are only a certain number of slots and participation is strictly enforced, but I'd love to have you:) To apply, please go here: http://lisalangblakeney.com/arc-reviewers/

BOOK LIST

The Masterson Series

Masterson

Masterson Unleashed

Masterson In Love

Joseph Loves Juliette

The King Brothers Series

Claimed

Indebted

Broken

Promised

The Nighthawk Series

Gunslinger

Wolf

Diesel

The Valencia Mafia Series

Rum Runners

ABOUT THE AUTHOR

Lisa Lang Blakeney is an international bestselling author of contemporary romance sold in more than 28 countries. Worried that her fellow PTO moms might disapprove, she wrote and published her steamy debut novel Masterson under a different title and pen name in August of 2015.

Thanks to strong reader support of her alpha male character, Roman Masterson, she was encouraged to continue with the series and published the entire Masterson Trilogy the following year. She hasn't looked back since and continues to write novels featuring strong alpha men and the smart women they seek to claim.

A romance junkie for sure, you can find Lisa watching a romantic comedy, reading a romance novel, or writing one of her own most days of the week. If she's not doing that, she's outside in the garden tending to her roses.

Lisa is the wife of one alpha (whom she met in college), mother to four girls, and two labradoodles. Get news on releases, sales and giveaways when you become one of Lisa's VIP readers at : http://LisaLangBlakeney.com/VIP